SPLIT SECOND

How Scotland won the World Cup in 1966

Martin Dey

This book is dedicated to my two older brothers, Graham and Alistair Dey who raised me in the lore of Scottish football in the 1960s and to my nearest in age brother, Johnny Dey who scored a great "Terry McDermott" drag back and chip from the edge of the box, when we played together for Cameron Athan Youth Club, Walthamstow in 1979.
Also in respectful memory of Jim Baxter and Jock Stein, the two principal characters in the story.

Split-Second

*Split second: How Scotland
won the World Cup in 1966*

A novel by Martin Dey

Prologue

The End Determines the Meaning.

We all know the story. Scotland had a Golden Generation of great players in the 1960's, playing for the top clubs in the English First Division and reaching European Finals, yet they underachieved at international level. Scotland in the 1960s did not reach a World Cup or European Championship Finals. One of the brightest stars of that decade, Jim Baxter, graced the world stage briefly between 1961 and 67, before self-inflicted damage through excessive booze and too little training, ended his career long before it should have. In all the years since the 1960s, no Scotland team has ever qualified from the group stage of a major competition, even though teams from equally small countries have achieved this. Now the rest of the world has passed Scotland by and children the world over, no longer remember that Scottish footballers were once among the best in the world.

Did that have to be the story?

In December 1964 Jim Baxter was riding the crest of a wave, driven by natural talent and supreme self-confidence. Multiple domestic honours, big wins in European competition (Borussia Monchengladbach 11-0, Wolves 3-1, Monaco 6-4, Seville 4-2, Red Star 8-6, Rapid Vienna 3-0) and in International football, Scotland had won 17 of the 24 matches that Baxter had played in, including three wins out of three against England and a 6-2 win against Spain in Madrid. The two games that Baxter played in the qualifying tournament for the 1966 World Cup were both won by Scotland, including victory over group favourites, Italy. In the four games he missed, Scotland beat only part-time Finland at home.

On 3rd December 1964 a frustrated and humiliated Austrian right half called Walter Skocik reacted to one Baxter nutmeg too many in the dying minutes of a European Cup tie in Vienna. The match was already long won by a superior Rangers team. Skocik launched a vengeful and premediated assault on Baxter's leg, shattering his career, robbing Rangers of their star player amidst a successful European run and robbing Scotland of Baxter's skills for crucial qualification games for the 1966 World Cup. Many of those who played with Baxter believe that he was never the same consistently influential player that he had been before the leg break.

What if Baxter hadn't broken his leg? If he continued to ride the crest of the wave? If top class matches twice a week sustained his natural fitness, compensating for his avoidance of training and excesses of drink? If he could have extended his ability to dominate and win football matches for 18 months more?

The 1966 World Cup was played in England. Had Scotland qualified they would have been the second best, perhaps even the best, supported team in the competition. Their top-class players would have been playing on grounds well familiar to them, within conditions even the SFA officials could not fail to master.

On 30th July 1966, if Walter Skocik had not broken Jim Baxter's leg, Scotland would have won the World Cup.

Split Second.

Baxter glides away from Skocik's lunge.

Ye either want tae gang doon this dreel or ye dinnae,ken?

Chapter 1

See they English, they cannae play nane

Every Scot has the date, 30th July 1966 forever enshrined in their heart. The memory vibrant and sweet, whether in black and white, colour or for the lucky 50,000 inside the stadium, raucous and intimate. Neither can we forget the hundreds of thousands flowing through the bars, streets and fountains of London like an exuberant tartan tide.

For the eleven that played that day the greatest prize. Immortality. Simpson, Greig, Gemmell, Murdoch, McNeil, McKinnon, Johnstone, Bremner, Gilzean, Law and Baxter.

Ten minutes before kick-off, Jim Baxter looks like he hasn't a care in the world, legs outstretched, face buried in the "Sporting Post". He lifts his head out of the newspaper and tells his teammates. "See they English, they cannae play nane. Player for player, across the park, we're better than them."

Big Jock Stein feels his chest tighten, a bead of sweat slips down his forehead. This is not the team talk he wants. This is not the blast against complacency his need for control demands. Every fiber of his being wants to interject and tell his players not to underestimate worthy opponents on their home turf in the final of their home tournament, in the biggest match of the 22 players lives. Instead, an older, deeper instinct takes over. He remembers Alan Gamble, the miner who walked out of a cave-in as if he was walking out of his own living room. "Whit took ye sae lang, lads?"

He lets Baxter's nonchalant show of fearlessness wash over the dressing room.

"No" thinks big Jock, "nonchalant is no' quite the right word. Gallus."

Chapter 2

Child of War

Our story begins in Austria, in Schwechat, an unassuming suburb south of Vienna. 15th March 1938, just days after Anschluss in announced,   Walter Skocik's father is one of the tens of thousands Austrians who line the streets of Vienna to cheer the Fuhrer's triumphal entry. The crowd flows into the Heldenplatz, some of the more athletic young Austrians climb onto the bronze rump of Prince Eugen's horse, for a better view of Adolf Hitler greeting his fellow countrymen from the balcony of the Hofburg Palace. 99.75% of voting age Austrians will vote in favour of union with Germany. Seven years later they will tell allied administrators that it was coerced expediency but it is likely that many are conveniently forgetting their enthusiasm for Greater Germany.

Schwechat is home to oil refineries and to the aircraft factory Heinkel-Sud, which grows in size and importance as the war progresses. More and more of Heinkel-Sud's war manufacturing takes place in cavernous tunnels, carved out by the emaciated slave labourers from the Mauthausen and Gusen concentration camps. Skeletal Czechs, Gypsies, Poles, German Socialists, even Spanish Republicans and in the final years of the war ever more Russians, Hungarians and Austrian Jews.

Walter was born in Schwechat on 6th September 1940. What a moment in time for Walter's parents to welcome their baby son. In September 1940 Greater Germany was sweeping all before it. Poland, Norway, Belgium, Holland and France all conquered. In the skies over England the Heinkel bombers that Schwechat's citizens helped to build were pulverizing the British airbases and cities into submission. It is difficult to imagine that Walter's parents did not envisage that a wonderful Germanic empire awaited their new born son.

In Austria there were only minor ripples of disquiet, before the storm broke in 1944. Many young Austrians went off to fight on the Russian front and on Walter's second birthday, Russian Pettyakov P-8 bombers dropped the first bombs on Vienna. The Russian planes required a 2,000 mile round trip to inflict little more than token damage. Southern Austria was similarly out of reach of British and American planes flying from England's bomber coast. Southern Austria was dubbed the "air raid shelter of the Reich". Heinkel -Sud grew larger and top-secret work progressed on the jet engines, that roared like dragons when they were tested in the caves and tunnels underground.

Then in June 1944 life changed for Walter and his family. For Austria it was not so much D-Day as the allied capture of Italy. Now British and American bombers could unleash on Austrian industrial targets, the punishment that Germany had been suffering for years. For young Walter the different Abwehr sirens must have become second nature. The intermittent whistle, like that of a cuckoo, signifying enemy planes airbourne, destination unknown, followed, ever more frequently, by the wailing siren of enemy bombers overhead. Within his shutzraum air raid shelter, four year old Walter, may have repeated the phrases he hears the adults say. "Englander schwein!" "Amerikaner schwein!"

Schwechat is a prime target. On 16th June American B-24 bombers of the 15th Airforce attack for the first time, with raids again on 10 September, 7th October, 7th February 1945, 14th February, 20th February and 15th March. Amid all this hell, Walter's parents know that an even greater horror is unfolding.

The Russians are pressing in on Vienna more quickly than the western allies.

Everyone had heard the stories of Russian atrocities, as the

Red Army advances. After the millions of Russian soldiers and civilians killed and after the brutality with which conquering German forces had treated them, it would be against human nature for the weary Soviet soldiers not to wish revenge. Four and a half year old Walter wants to be strong but he can sense the fear in his parents' voices, the anxiety etched into their faces. Walter's father is fearful that a Russian soldier doesn't like his face or likes his wife's too much. As March turns to April Gauleiter Von Schirach declares that Vienna and the surrounding suburbs are a fortress of the Reich and calls on all Volksstrum and Hitler Youth to join the few remaining SS Panzer Units in a final defiant defence. Supplies of electricity, gas and water have broken down, as has all civilian authority. The family has become used to living in the cellar, feeding off scraps. "Wir bleiben hier unten verborgen, eh mein Kind?"

"We keep ourselves hidden down here, eh my child?" Walter's father tells his little soldier. "Ja, Papa" Walter replies.

By 15th April Vienna and the surrounding area has fallen to the Soviet Army, six months of fear, deprivation and uncertainty follow. Then in November, news of great joy, their home is to be in the British sector of the four-power division of the Reich. The airfield used by Heinkel-Sud becomes RAF Schwechat, an important base for allied planes during the Berlin airlift, as cold war tensions rise in 1948

April 1955, Walter is a 14 year-old solid and combative footballer, as the four occupying powers pull out. Austria becomes its own country once again. Neither Anschluss nor occupied and blessedly, not within the Communist Bloc.

RAF Schwechat becomes Vienna International Airport, onto whose runway Glasgow Rangers will land in December 1964, to play Rapid Vienna in the European Cup. Stepping onto the tarmac is 25 year old Rangers skipper, Jim Baxter, with 24-year-old Walter Skocik , waiting nearby to play in the Rapid Vienna side.

Chapter3

I am who I bloody well am!

"I am speaking to you from the cabinet room at 10 Downing Street. This morning the British ambassador in Berlin handed the German government a final note stating that unless we heard from them by 11 o'clock that they were prepared at once to withdraw their troops from Poland, a state of war would exist between us. I have to tell you now that no such undertaking has been received, and that consequently this country is at war with Germany. We have a clear conscience, we have done all that any country could do to establish peace, but a situation in which no word given by Germany's ruler could be trusted, and no people or country could feel itself safe has become intolerable. Now may God bless you all and may He defend the right. For it is the evil things that we shall be fighting against, brute force, bad faith, injustice, oppression, and persecution. And against them I am certain that the right will prevail."

At fifteen minutes past eleven on the 3rd September 1939 radio listeners across the United Kingdom hear the mournful, regret-laden words of Prime Minister Neville Chamberlain. The British Government has been desperate to avoid war, the memory of the mechanized slaughter of the Great War is still so very raw. So many families, so many communities sacrificed their sons and husbands, it seems inconceivable that Germany, who lost two million soldiers, does not have the same aversion to a second war only twenty-one years after the first.

Every community in Britain has sacrificed and across the land war memorials stand as lasting reminders of the horrendous cost of war. In the tiny Fife village of Lumphinnans, seventy names are inscribed on the memorial, including that of Robert Baxter, a footballer for Raith Rovers before the war, who died in 1915. Baxter had served with distinction in the Boer War and in 1914 volunteered for the 2nd Battalion of the Black Watch, Royal Highlanders, at Cowdenbeath. Private Baxter 3/3977 arrived in France on 22 April 1915. Exactly 3 weeks later, on 13 May, he was killed in action in the trenches, where his experience and courage under fire counted for almost nothing amid the murderous artillery and machine guns of the First World War.

Robert left behind a widow, Elizabeth, and two young sons, Rab and David. After the war, Elizabeth marries for the second time, with James Curran becoming stepfather to the Baxter boys. In 1920 Elizabeth and James have a daughter, also called Elizabeth. Both Rab and David are good footballers and tragically their stepfather dies in 1934 while watching David play for St Johnstone.

As world-wide tensions increased in January 1939, eighteen-year-old Elizabeth Curran takes up with Robert Moffat and falls pregnant out of wedlock. On 29th September Elizabeth gives birth to a baby boy, named James Curran, in honour of her father. War intervenes once more. Robert Moffat is posted overseas with the RAF. Feeling the pressure of being an unmarried mother, young Elizabeth agrees to a family plan to give her young baby to older half-brother Rab and his wife Agnes, who have been unable to have a child of their own. Throughout her life, Elizabeth experiences regret at her decision, expressed perhaps most poignantly by the secret scrapbook she keeps of newspaper cuttings following the career of her son, now renamed, James Curran Baxter.

These are proud and stoical people. A decision has been made; an agreement of sorts has been concluded. Part of the agreement is that young Jim is not to be told the truth of his origins. Despite continuing to live in close proximity, all parties stick to the agreement, Rab and Aggy fervently protecting the family they have created. Elizabeth, with Robert returned from the war, abiding, with quiet resignation, that they should not rock the boat and dislocate Jim from the family he has come to know as his own. Elizabeth and Robert marry and have three further children. Jim knows them as cousins, the children of his aunty Betty. The two families are not encouraged to be close.

Except the boat is rocked. In a small mining community, young Jim may not know the truth but everyone else does. Aged 12 Jim reacts when an older boy fouls him in a village kick-about. "Ach, ye dirty bastard!" Jim exclaims. "Naw, ye're the bastard, Baxter." The youth replies. After the match, Jim asks his mother Aggy to explain the meaning of the words. Jim is told a terse version of the truth. He was abandoned as a baby and adopted by Rab and Aggy. The family of three closes in and the subject appears to be closed. Jim, Rab and Aggy remain devoted throughout their lives. Years later a modern-day psychiatrist wonders if perhaps a part of Jim's psyche converts this uncertainty into a life-long desire to live for the moment. Jim experiences an extra sense of freedom from excelling at football. From being himself. From being the best. He can skip over tackles and in that moment float above the unanswered questions about his past. "I am who I bloody well am! I always have been. I always will be. I'm James Curran Baxter and I'll live my life my way and nae other!"

Chapter 4

Collision Course.

Jim's journey to Vienna.

R ab and Agg Baxter raise Jim in the west Fife village of Hill o' Beath. The village is dominated by Fordell Colliery, where Rab works. The colliery had been owned by the Duke of Buckingham and boasted Lady Anne, George and the humorously titled, William Pitt but since 1945 Fordell, like all other mines, is now run by the National Coal Board, as the commanding heights of industrial production are taken under Public Ownership. If every Scottish village had at its heart a War Memorial with a disproportionate number of names from 1914-18, every Miners' Social Club had a book of remembrance. For Fordell there were 32 names, recording the fatalities since mining started in 1843. This includes the three young lassies, pithead sorters who separated coal from stone, who were dreadfully scalded and killed by a boiler explosion in 1876. Other miners have died in roof and slab falls, cage and shaft accidents and trolley escapes.

The miners work hard and play hard. Gambling schools in the Social Clubs and great numbers from mining communities showing skills as footballers. The Ayrshire village of Glenbuck is famous for producing 53 professional footballers, including the great Liverpool manager, Bill Shankly. Fife's mining communities produce scores of players for the local senior teams Dunfermline, Raith Rovers and Cowdenbeath and also for the juniors. The teams may have been called Primrose and Violet but the tackling is hard and the language rarely flowery.

A teenage Jim Baxter is playing three-card brag in the Hill o' Beath Institute when his friend Malcolm Sinclair comes in to persuade him to join him in a game for Halbeath Boys Club. Jim calls to see the other hands and loses all his money. On a turn of the cards his football career begins. Six months later he signs for Crossgate Primrose and from there Raith Rovers, a team, at the time, in the top half of the Scottish First Division. Raith manager, Bert Herdman sees that Jim's balance, control and passing make him an ideal attacking wing-half. "Show for the ball, pass and show for the ball again" is Herdman's simple but effective advice. Soon Herdman's team-talk becomes, "Give the ball to Jim."

Two months after Jim's twentieth birthday he plays a great game, scoring one and making two, as Raith stun Rangers as they come back from two goals down to win 3-2 at Ibrox. Rangers' manager, Scott Symon vows to sign Jim, paying a record transfer fee between Scottish clubs of £17,500, with the signing being announced on 24th April 1960 the day Rangers beat Kilmarnock in the Scottish Cup Final.

In the spring of 1960, the paths of Walter Skocik and Jim Baxter almost cross for the first time. Baxter was under consideration by the selectors of the Scotland team but he is not chosen for an end of season tour of Austria, Hungary and Turkey. Nineteen-year old Walter Skocik has broken through into the Rapid Vienna first team and plays right half for the Austrians on 29th May when they defeat a disappointing Scottish side 4-0. Baxter does make his international debut in November that year in a 5-2 victory over Northern Ireland. Baxter's first appearance was Scotland's only victory amid a dreadful run of results, in which Baxter played no part, which saw defeats to Austria, Poland, Turkey and Wales and reached its lowest point on 15th April 1961 when Scotland are humiliated 9-3 by England at Wembley

Baxter soon establishes himself in Glasgow as Rangers' playmaker, the starting point of so many attacks and goals. Domestic honours flow in, the League Cup won in October 1960, the 1960-61 League clinched in April. His first season also sees a strong European run, with Rangers reaching the final of the European Cup Winners Cup. May 1961 is a busy month for Jim. On 3rd and 7th May Scotland began their World Cup qualification campaign with home and away victories over Ireland. 14th May sees defeat in Bratislava to main section rivals, Czechoslovakia, followed on 17th and 27th May by the home and away defeats to Fiorentina in the Cup Winners Cup Final

All this is achieved while Jim is also completing two years of National Service in the Army. Baxter is one of the very last men to be conscripted with the cut off coming two days after his birthday. He is allocated to the Black Watch, the same Regiment that Robert Baxter, senior, had fought and died in forty-five years before. Baxter mostly serves guard duty in Stirling Castle, which keeps him close enough to join up with his Rangers' team mates on matchdays. Baxter also plays several games for the Army, including a game in March '61 where the Army pulled rank on Rangers and refused to release him for a Scottish Cup replay with Motherwell, which Rangers go on to lose. Overall, being in the Army and playing football twice a week is good for Jim Baxter, as even in his first season with Rangers, he is establishing a reputation as a poor trainer and a heavy drinker. Jim's whole career becomes a battle between his natural fitness, ability and confidence and the growing detrimental effect of a lifestyle that is to prove unhealthy for a sportsman and human being both. In the years of Baxter's early to mid-twenties, as long as Jim is playing regularly, he manages to keep on the right side of the battle. Once he breaks his leg the balance begins to shift toward the eroding effects of too much excess. The massive self-belief and Jim's determination to live his life his own way, mean that he is never going to submit to a manager's authority or knuckle down to training. The confidence and skill walk hand in hand with the self-destructive drinking and gambling. You can imagine what Jim Baxter might have done if he hadn't broken his leg but you can't imagine what might have happened if he had bowed to authority and accepted a lifestyle not of his own choosing. That person simply wouldn't be Jim Baxter. His great strength and his great weakness both stem from being his own man.

****

In 61-62, Jim's second season with Rangers, there are victories in the League Cup and Scottish Cup. Once again Jim misses a cup tie against Motherwell because the British Army need him to play against the Belgian Army. This time his Rangers teammates manage to win without him and Jim plays in the Final against St. Mirren. The League title is lost to Dundee, with Rangers picking up only seven points from their last seven games. Rangers reach the Quarter Final of the European Cup but lose 4-3 on aggregate to Standard Liege, the match in Glasgow being missed by Rangers' young winger, Willie Henderson because he gets stuck in traffic.

After Scotland beat Czechoslovakia 3-2 at Hampden in September 61, a play-off is needed between the two teams level on points. Leading the play-off 2-1, Scotland come within seven minutes of qualifying for the 1962 World Cup and are denied only by a shot which strikes the bar and bounces out. Scottish goalkeeper, Eddie Connachan and Right-Half Pat Crerand are both sure the ball did not cross the line but the Belgian referee gives the goal. There are cameras at the play-off between Scotland and Czechoslovakia but there is no known remaining footage of this 83rd minute shot, to judge if it was a goal or not. The Czechs go on to reach the World Cup Final, briefly leading before Brazil beat them 3-1. On 14th April 1962 Jim Baxter plays against England for the first time. The Scots restore some pride, after the 9-3 defeat the year before, with a 2-0 win. Baxter is to play for Scotland against England five times and only once is he not on the winning side.

1962-63 sees two months of football lost to a freezing winter and the season extended into May. Rangers regain the League title

15

and win the Scottish Cup, beating Celtic 3-0 in the final. Europe once again ends with disappointment with a comprehensive 8-4 aggregate defeat to Spurs. It is with the Scottish national side that Jim really begins to be recognized as a World Class player. On April 6th 1963, at Wembley, Jim produces one of his most memorable performances, scoring twice as England are beaten 2-1. The second goal is a penalty. Baxter had no track record as a penalty taker but his self-belief is so high that Dave MacKay simply throws the ball to him and he slots it home past Gordon Banks. This victory is achieved with only ten men with Scottish Captain, Eric Caldow, having his leg broken by Bobby Smith after only five minutes. Jim Baxter loves the big match atmosphere of Wembley. "This is the London Palladium. If I don't turn it on here, then you can kick me up the backside after the game" he told journalists before the match.

One month later, Austria come to Hampden with Walter Skocik not in the team. Scotland are leading 4-1 against a very aggressive Austrian team, who have two players sent off before the referee takes the extraordinary step of abandoning the game after 79 minutes, to prevent any further serious foul play. A month after that, on 13th June 1963, Jim is part of the Scotland team that defeats Spain 6-2 in Madrid. "This is one of the greatest teams ever to wear the Scottish jersey. They were all magnificent- no superb. On this form we would have beaten the best side in the world" comments manager Ian McColl. Hopes are high for the qualifying group for the 1966 World Cup.

• •

1963-64 is a great season for Jim Baxter, Rangers and Scotland. Rangers win the domestic treble, beating rivals Celtic in 5 games out of five in all competitions, scoring 11 goals and conceding one. The only disappointment for Rangers, in 63-64, is in Europe where a heavy defeat to Real Madrid puts them out the European Cup in the first round. Despite a promising display in the home leg, both Baxter and Rangers find that they still have a lot to learn when playing Europe's finest.

In the four games Baxter plays for Scotland that season, they beat Norway 6-1, Wales 2-1, England 1-0 and draw 2-2 with West Germany in Hanover. At that point West Germany have never beaten Scotland, with two wins to the Scots and this draw. The German newspaper "Die Welt" declares "German footballers simply cannot win against the Scots".

In October 1963 Baxter's growing world recognition is acknowledged when he is selected for the FIFA World XI to play England in a match to commemorate the centenary of the English FA. Baxter plays alongside stars such as Alfredo Di Stefano, Ferenc Puskas, Eusebio, Uwe Seeler, Raymond Kopa and Josef Masopust. One issue that deeply troubles Jim Baxter is how little he gets paid by Rangers, compared to these players or compared to the English based players in the Scotland team. Rangers have a rigid wage structure and Directors who would rather sell their prize asset than release more money to help the team compete with their European rivals. Two pre-seasons in a row Baxter backs down from threats not to sign a new contract. He will not back down forever.

• •

And so, to season 64-65, which is to see Baxter and Rangers travel to Vienna in December. The pre-season is blighted by the tragic death of John White of Tottenham and Scotland. White had been struck by lightning while sheltering from a storm, under a tree on a golf course. White, like Baxter, was a vital part of Scotland's midfield and, at only 27, was expected to play a crucial role in Scotland's World Cup campaign. John White leaves a wife and two small children.

Despite their treble success the previous season, 64-65 does not start well for Rangers. On October 17th with 8 games played Rangers are in 10th place with only seven points. Part of the reason is that the Scottish league of the mid 60s is highly competitive. In 13 seasons from 1952 to 65, seven different teams win the Scottish League. Scottish football is also a force to be reckoned with in European club football. Here is a Magnificent Seven of results from the 60s: Dundee 8 Cologne1, Kilmarnock 7 Antwerp 2, Dunfermline 6 Valencia 2, Hibs 5 Napoli 0, Rangers 8 Borussia Monchengladbach 0, Dundee United 2 Barcelona 0, Celtic 2 Inter Milan 1.

These are not freak results. Scottish teams are consistently good in European competition. From 1959-60 to 1969-70 there is a Scottish team in at least the Quarter Final of a European tournament every season. One triumph, two finalists, 8 semi-finalists and four quarter-finalists in this period. All this being achieved while a steady stream of top players move to play in England. In 1964 Kilmarnock beat Eintracht Frankfurt 5-1 in the Fairs Cup. In the same tournament Dunfermline knock out Stuttgart. Rangers can expect stiff competition not only from Celtic but from the top eight teams in Scotland.

Mid-October and a corner appears to be turned for Baxter and Rangers. On 21st October Baxter is in the Scotland team that starts the World Cup qualification campaign with a 3-1 win over Finland. Three days later, Baxter captains Rangers to victory over Celtic in front of 91,000 fans in the League Cup Final. Young Jim Forrest scoring two goals with Jimmy Johnstone countering for Celtic. A week later Forrest scores another double as Rangers knock Red Star Belgrade out of the European Cup. Away Goals do not yet count double in Europe, so this victory was in a play-off after a 5-5 aggregate tie. Baxter dictates the play that night and at last Rangers appear to have developed tactics to break down strong European defences.

Rangers climb the league table to sixth with a six game unbeaten run and on November 18th, Rapid Vienna, with Walter Skocik at right half, come to Ibrox in the European Cup. Rapid opt for ten man defence, which Rangers breach only once when a pass from Jim Baxter sends Davy Wilson through to score.

Chapter 5

Split Second.

14.44pm December 8th.

Prater Stadion, Vienna.

T here has been snowfall in the days before Rangers arrive in Vienna. 70,000 tickets have been sold for the match, so the army is called in to help clear the pitch. Rain falls on the morning of the 8th creating a slushy playing surface. The Austrians are a physical, well-drilled team, playing the offside trap and breaking forward from a solid defence. They are confident they can overturn the one goal deficit from the first leg.

Rangers are also confident. Davy Wilson recalls, "I had a feeling that we would win the game in Vienna. There was no way that I thought it was going to be easy because Rapid were a strong and a very experienced team but we were starting to learn some lessons about European football by that time and I had a feeling that if we played as well as we had in Glasgow then we would go through. Baxter was sensational. He wasn't bothered about the mud and mush below his feet. His confidence was higher than ever and , believe me, that was no mean feat but he turned on all his tricks and enjoyed every minute of the match until the last."

Baxter dictates play from the beginning, with the ability to either release the ball early or hold it away from opponents long enough for the forwards to stay onside. In 19 minutes just such a well-timed pass sends Jim Forrest through to score. Alex Willoughby remembers, "The performance Jim gave in Vienna in that second game against Rapid was one of the finest one-man performances I have ever seen in a game at that level. We are talking about the Austrian champions as opposition and Rapid were rated as one of the top teams on the Continent then and he was at his very best. Baxter took everything that was going that day except for the gate money and the way he played they should have given that to him. The Austrian players could not do anything to stop him until the last minute of the game. He was captain that day. The tie was won and all Jim had to do with the ball was lift it to the back of the terracings, get it out of play and wait for the referee's final whistle but he always had a different outlook from most other players. He was just so good and used to inviting tackles and then stepping away from them, still keeping the ball."

Ten minutes into the second half and Rapid winger Schmid crunches into Eric Caldow, causing him to be taken off for treatment. Poor Eric has an unlucky record of playing against Smiths or Schmids! Despite being down to ten men, Willie Johnston breaks through the Rapid defence and squares the ball to Davy Wilson, who makes the score 2-0. Bobby Shearer recalls, "Jim always had that bit of arrogance or cheek if you like, about him and when you played the game the way he did you needed that. Now in Vienna he had been absolutely magnificent, the best I had ever seen him play and that was saying a lot. Then he gained possession right at the end of the game and took the ball round this poor fellow who had been trying to mark him all afternoon, then he went back and took it round him again and when he did it for a third time the lad just cracked and lunged into the tackle. He had had enough of Jim taking the mickey out of him."

Jim Baxter takes up the story, "We were enjoying ourselves, we really were. When we went out, they couldn't cope with us. There was some slush on top of the pitch and that was absolutely made for me, believe it or not. Their defenders couldn't turn on it, so I kept pinging the ball round them. You showed them the ball and once they made their commitment they couldn't stop. Their right-half was Walter Skocik and he must have had the worst day of his career. I just kept nutmegging him. I don't know how many balls I put through his legs. It must have been dozens-I lost count. I'll tell you how good we were- the Rapid supporters were throwing snowballs at their own players. Not only that, they had started cheering us. We were nearing the final whistle and I knew that there wasn't long to go, so I started walking toward the dressing room. I turned round and asked for the ball."

Davy Wilson: "The big guy, Skocik, was hunting Baxter down, charging about in a rage. I shouted for the ball to take it into the corner and kill some time but Jim was either not listening or he wasn't finished making a fool out of the Rapid team. Thirty seconds to go of a great team performance, with a great result."

Ronnie McKinnon: "Baxter was in sensational form that night in Vienna. He was taking the mickey out of the guy Skocik who was one of Rapid's star players. Baxter could do that to anybody. Skocik got annoyed and frustrated. Baxter put the ball through the guy's legs for the umpteenth time and walked round him and the player chased him. The Rapid player just couldn't take any more punishment from Baxter. No matter who the opposition were, if Rangers were in trouble at the back we just gave the ball to Baxter. He demanded the ball anyway. Baxter had no nerves and myself and John Greig just gave him the ball when the pressure was on so we could have a rest in defence. At times we just stood back in awe and admired his talent. More often than not he'd dribble away up to the other end and the ball would end up in the opponents' net."

Split second.

The second splits. 14.44 pm December 8th 1964. Prater Stadion, Vienna. 89 minutes into the match. In one reality the final whistle is blown with Jim Baxter lying in agony on the pitch with a broken leg. In the other, Baxter jumps over Skocik's lunge and it is Walter who lies in a disconsolate heap by the touchline. Baxter goes on, confidence, skill and fitness higher than ever.

Riding the crest of the wave.

Chapter 6

Captain Baxter

December 1964

J ubilant, if a little worse for wear following the after-match banquet with Rapid players and staff, the Rangers travelling party is on a coach heading for Salzburg, because Vienna airport is closed due to thick fog. Man of the match, Jim Baxter, is holding court at the back of the bus. "Haw Tottie, you speak German, whit does this newspaper wi' ma picture on it, say about me?"

Rangers Icelandic inside-left Thorolf Beck studies the broadsheet "Kronen Zeitung". Beck can speak Icelandic, Danish, English and German. He reads carefully, "Rapid were beaten by a very fine team and also by a truly world-class player in Jim Baxter"

Baxter cheers. Most of his team-mates, the younger ones especially, cheer with him. "Go on, Tottie, whit else?" Baxter demands. Beck reads "On this form, only Pele can be rated as Baxter's equal."

"Ho!" Baxter calls out "Ye hear that, Mr Symon!? Now gie me equal pay wi' Pele! Ken, after the match, I wis speaking tae Skocik, the big lad, who tried tae whack me and he's on mair money than I am. A player who's no even quick enough tae foul me!"

Up in the front seats, director John Lawrence, face like thunder, ticks another black mark against Baxter's long list of misdemeanors. Humiliating disrespect in front of the full staff. Next to him manager Scot Symon squirms in his seat. He has built his team and all his recent success round Baxter but he finds it increasingly difficult to convince the board that the rewards outweigh the affronts. Symon would find the money to keep his star player but it is not his money to find. "Shut him up, Scot, for decency sake." Lawrence whispers insistently to his manager.

Symon cannot risk a public confrontation. He knows how hard it is to mold Jim Baxter to club discipline, no matter who is watching. Symon speaks in low tones to trainer Davie Kinnear, who moves uncertainly down the jolting bus in search of the ebullient, yet discontented, star.

Kinnear tries to impart his words as privately as possible in a crowded coach. "Jim, this is serious. You're no tae discuss money in front of the Directors. You know Mr Symon is doing all he can for you. Mouthing aff in public like this will no help your case. You've been given free reign tae dae your newspaper column and we know all about all they bar tabs at the Club's expense at the St. Enoch's. Just pipe doon, eh?"

Despite repeatedly dodging his training, Baxter has instinctive sympathy for Kinnear's task as messenger boy, he smiles as he places his hand on Kinnear's shoulder. His words are conciliatory, yet deliberately loud enough for those nearby to hear. "Aw right you are, Davie. Now that I ken the bar tabs are official, it's straight tae the St Enoch's I'll be going when we get hame!"

Kinnear shrugs his shoulders to Symon as he returns to his seat. The back of the bus has broken into a chorus of "As I was walking down the Copeland Road"

"Mr Lawrence," Symon pleads, still trying to lift the thunder from his Director's brow, "we have a European Cup Quarter Final coming up. We need all out best players."

Lawrence turns to face Symon. It is less than 24 hours since one of the greatest individual European performances in the club's history. "Very well, Mr Symon but as soon as this European run is over, Baxter goes on the transfer list."

****

Another manager under pressure is Scot Symon's former teammate, Scotland Manager, Ian McColl. McColl has to work with a press that inflates Scotland's ability, while being unreasonably dismissive of the opposition. The 2-2 away draw with West Germany is described by the Glasgow Herald as a "most unsatisfactory international match and rightly neither side ended

as winners." This is followed on October 3rd when the Scots give away two goals in the last five minutes to lose 3-2 to Wales. McColl comes up with the same solution as Scot Symon; make Jim Baxter captain. Despite his lack of discipline off the field, Baxter is well suited to being captain. Leading either club or country out in front of a huge crowd suits his swagger. On the playing field Baxter desperately wants to win and, where possible, win well, to show his superiority. His game is about unlocking opposition defences and it helps him develop a shrewd tactical brain. When he captains Rangers to victory in the League Cup Final, he spots that Celtic wingers Johnstone and Hughes have swapped wings, so Baxter switches his full-backs, Provan and Caldow, to ensure that big John Hughes continues to have the more physical Davie Provan up against him.

Amid the drama of Rangers European run, Baxter captains Scotland to three victories in a month. First is the World Cup victory over Finland, where some fans stay to jeer because Scotland have not added to a 3 goal half time lead. "It's a win. That's all that counts." McColl tersely tells the papers.

Next, McColl takes his players to London for an emotionally charged testimonial game for John White against Tottenham. Scotland win 6-2, with Dundee's Alan Gilzean scoring twice, goals which help persuade Spurs to sign him. Tom White of Hearts, John's brother, scores for Spurs.

Two weeks later, on 25th November Baxter captains Scotland to a 3-2 win over Northern Ireland, the first time Baxter and 18 year old George Best share a pitch.

When it is remembered that the play-off with Red Star and the two legs against Rapid Vienna also take place in this month, it is further proof that Jim Baxter operates best when playing big games only days apart. Not only providing playing as an antidote to not training but also minimizing time for late nights and drinking. For a man who might be described now as having undiagnosed ADHD, the more successful he is for club and country, the more important games he plays: the less time he has for mischief.

Chapter 7

Hello, Mister Herrera
February/March 1965

Sportswriter William McIlvaney writes in his newspaper column, "It is as if Rangers have grown tired of the monotony and small-beer of the domestic season. Even the tribal festival enacted on January 1st, where Celtic were beaten once again, was a muted affair. All eyes at Ibrox are set toward Europe and the journey on 17th February to the San Siro Stadium for their European Cup Quarter Final first leg against Helenio Herrera's Inter Milan. I can express this change of focus in no stronger terms than when I say that there are some of a Rangers persuasion, players and supporters both, who would trade a win over Celtic for a good result in Milan."

One man who is definitely up for such a trade is Rangers captain Jim Baxter. "Though I dinnae see why we cannae dae both?" is his typically confident reply.

There is talk in the papers that Herrera has told Italian journalists that Baxter is a player he would like to sign. Scot Symon calls Baxter to his office and explains that this is just part of Herrera's legendary mind-games designed to make Jim deviate from his usual performance by trying too hard to impress. "Maybe so boss," Baxter replies, "I'll play my ain game, whether he wants tae sign me or no."

Symon is reassured that Baxter's reply is the straightforward truth. In his gut he remains worried that Inter may really want to take away his star man.

Scotland may have sacrificed in the two World Wars but it did not experience the twentieth century dislocation and devastation that engulfed mainland Europe. A world that threw up the wandering Magyars, Puskas and Kubala. A world that produced Herrera. The son of an Andalucian anarchist who fled to Buenos Aires. Herrera returned to Europe via Morocco and occupied France. Like many great managers he was not a great footballer and injury pushed him into management at an early age. After a spell in France he took over at Atletico Madrid and led them to two La Liga titles. Barcelona followed with two titles, alongside two victories in the European Fairs Cup. In 1960 Herrera moved to Inter Milan and led them first to the Seria A title in 1962-63, followed by a European Cup win, 3-1 in the final over Real Madrid. Ominously for Rangers, this was the same Real who had beaten them 7-0 on aggregate earlier in the competition. Adding to Herrera's reputation, in September 1964 Inter won the Intercontinental Cup beating Independiente of Argentina.

Rangers are facing the Champions of the World.

Herrera is a modern manager. Old school managers like Scot Symon wear suits and rarely get involved with the details of training, nor have they control over signings, where the board still holds sway. Herrera insists on control over every aspect of team building, which players are signed, training routines, match tactics and underpinning everything, a detailed lifestyle regime for all players, to maximise their fitness in preparation for matchdays. The eating, drinking and carousing activities of players are strictly monitored through a network of informants and medical tests. Herrera drums a mantra into his players heads, "He who does not give everything, gives nothing."

Herrera is so influential that two aspiring Scottish managers fly to Milan in the 1963 close season. Jock Stein of Dunfermline and Willie Waddell of Kilmarnock watch and learn from the training and tactics.

In January 1965 Herrera places a call to Guiseppe Cabrelli an Italian businessman in Glasgow to ask what he knows of Jim

Baxter. "A sublime player, Mago" Cabrelli replies, "but a terrible athlete. He does not look after himself. Drinks, smokes and gambles too much."

"Can he change? For the chance to play for Inter? Would he change for me?" Herrera asks. The phone line goes quiet for a second as Cabrelli ponders. "No, Mago." Cabrelli replies, thinking back to the times he has seen Baxter stagger out of his restaurant on the night before a game. "Grazie" Herrera replies.

Herrera has perfected the catenaccio. A match tactic based on solid, whole team defence but also swift counter attacking, often through overlapping fullbacks. Giancinto Facchetti and Tarcisio Burgnich, able to go beyond the forwards due to the cover provided by Armando Picchi, the sweeper, filling any gap in defence. To flight the balls to the overlapping fullbacks Herrera brings Luis Suarez with him from Barcelona.

"Class+Preparation+Intelligence+Athleticism=Champions" Herrera's Inter prepare to take on Baxter's Rangers.

Rangers do prepare for the match. Jim Baxter, no lover of authority or rigid game plans, has enough of a football brain to know that Rangers can't just go into this match as they would a game against Clyde. He has said as much himself after the thrashing by Real. Scot Symon sits the players down and tells them they are going to mark Inter, man for man. "Willie, Davy," he says to the wingers Henderson and Wilson, "that means if Facchetti or Burgnich go forward, you go with them. Jimmy, you follow Suarez everywhere." Baxter heaves a sigh of relief as he realizes Symon is speaking to inside forward Jimmy Millar. Symon sees the twitch of a smile on Baxter's lips. "Jimmy, you go with their young inside-right, Mazzola." Symon fixes his gaze on Baxter. "Man for man is a whole team responsibility, remember. If one man in the opponent's team is allowed to go free, the whole system will fall. You're captain, Jimmy. This is our plan, right?" Symon stares at his captain, waiting for a response. After just a second too long, Baxter replies, "Aye, boss."

For the first 45 minutes the plan works like a dream. Rangers are not their usual free flowing selves but neither are Inter getting the freedom to create many chances. 0-0 at half time. The highest praise you could give the Ibrox side is to say it has been like a match between two Italian sides. Scot Symon is delighted, "Same again in the second half" is his team talk.

What goes wrong is perhaps bad luck rather than indiscipline. A crazy two minutes just three minutes after the re-start. Peiro shoots and the ball strikes Millar on the head. Millar drops to the ground but so does the ball, right to the feet of Suarez who volleys it with technical perfection into the back of the net. "Stick tae the plan!" Captain Baxter shouts as Rangers kick off but the goal has rattled them, possession is lost, Inter pour forward, Corso cuts inside Provan and shoots, well wide, for the left hand corner of the net. Peiro doesn't head the ball, it simply crashes off his head because the shot is so wayward. The ball ends up in the net. Rangers are two nil down.

Baxter picks the ball out of the net. The Inter players are running back to their end celebrating. Baxter is captain. He knows that panic has set in. He puts his foot on the ball on the edge of the eighteen yard box. "Lads, lads!" he shouts, demanding everyone's attention. "We can still dae this! Just fuckin' get a grip!"

From this re-start Baxter takes the ball for a wander, playing one-twos with Greig and Brand. The team settles down. Without consulting the manager, Baxter shouts, "We play our ain way, lads". Rangers open up. Within minutes Baxter puts Forrest through but he shoots wide. Attacking the Italians actually relieves pressure on the defence and players like Provan , Caldow, Greig and McKinnon can still get a tackle in when required. Just after the hour, Baxter chips Forrest through again and this time the young striker scores. It is the last goal of the game.

2-1 away is not a bad result. 1-0 at home will force a play-off. 2-0 at home, a place in the European Cup semi-finals.

****

The match at the San Siro had been watched by 50,000 fans. The return at Ibrox on 3rd March draws in a phenomenal 77,000. In his Sunday Mirror, ghost-written, column the week before, Jim Baxter urges the Ibrox faithful to roar Rangers to victory. The words are his own. "We are a match for the best in the World and on Wednesday we aim to prove it"

All the great and good of Scottish Society are in attendance, Sean Connery, the world's most famous actor. Jim Clark, the Formula One Racing Champion and rival football managers, Jock Stein and Willie Waddell, the two men who flew to Madrid to study Herrera. For all that these men are managers of the top and fourth teams in the Scottish First Division, it is widely speculated that their sights are set elsewhere. Stein has already agreed to leave Hibs after less than one season, to become Celtic's first ever Protestant manager, provided he has full control over team matters in the same way Herrera has. Waddell is said to view Kilmarnock as a steppingstone, as he hovers like a vulture over any Rangers manager. Also in the crowd are Dave MacKay and Bill Nicholson of Spurs. MacKay has always got on well with Baxter, on and off the park and hopes to persuade his boss that Jim is the man to replace the aging Danny Blanchflower in the Tottenham side.

Herrera, meantime, tells the Glasgow Press that Suarez has a heavy cold and may not play, even though Herrera knows it is little more than a sniffle.

Jim Baxter has heard rumours that the Board will not countenance any request for a wage increase at the end of his contract at season's end. He broods over the stories of interest from Inter and Spurs. He is engaged to beautiful Jean Ferguson and wants to buy them both a house, not something he can easily afford off the £45 a week Rangers pay him, well, not after his losses at the bar, cassino and bookies are deducted.

Most chillingly of all, Baxter has heard rumours that the Board will sell him as soon as Rangers are beaten in Europe. It is a contradictory and perplexing incentive. Only his natural desire to prove he is the best, drives him on. Baxter doesn't want to leave Rangers but he is a man who thrives on being loved and though he knows he is loved by the fans, most of the players and by Mr Symon, he doesn't feel loved by the Board.

For a man who doesn't know whom he should call his real mother, it is an emotionally charged conundrum, as he laces up his boots to face Inter Milan.

Yet when Jim leads his team out onto the Ibrox pitch, into the cauldron of noise, alongside the sleek, tanned, movie-star good looking Italians, he knows this is where he is meant to be. Where all doubt is banished and Slim Jim comes alive. Being Captain of Rangers matters too. Aged 25 he is older than Provan, Greig, McKinnon, Henderson, McLean, Forrest and Johnston playing alongside him. He only has to glance at 18 year old Willie Johnston, a fellow south-west Fifer from Cardenden and he feels like the big brother he has never had the chance to be. "You'll be alright, Bud" he tells the outside left as he ruffles his hair.

Rangers are a young, skillful and athletic side but Baxter gives them an extra edge. More than his footballing ability, it is his absolute self-confidence, his arrogance, that refuses to be cowed by any opposition. To believe he is as good as, or better than the World Champions. "C'mom lads," he calls, "it's only Inter we're playing!"

Roared on by the crowd, Rangers take an early lead. A Greig twenty yard shot is spilled by Sarti and Jim Forrest stabs the ball home. Rangers now have at least a play-off but Jim has heard the clubs have agreed a Spanish neutral venue and he doesn't fancy a match with a ref who knows Herrera from his days in Spain. In 69 minutes big George "Dandy" McLean cracks a great shot against the underside of the bar. Minutes later Guarneri barges Millar off the ball in the penalty box but the referee waves play on. Time is running out. Henderson and Johnston have had little change out of the Inter fullbacks, until three minutes from time. Baxter spins a ball down the line for Johnston to chase. For once he beats

Burgnich and gets in a cross. Picchi is there at the near post to cut it out but his touch is heavy and in a moment reminiscent of Baxter's goal against England two years previously, Jim nicks the ball and curls it into the top corner of Sarti's goal.

Bedlam. Rangers ride out the last three frantic minutes. Ecstasy, hugged by teammates and fans alike, Jim has found the love and affirmation his soul needs.

Jim shakes hands with Helenio Herrera. "Hello Mister Herrera," he says with a grin, "d'you still want tae sign me?". Herrera replies with a dignified, "Well played" but cannot help thinking he can smell Bacardi off Baxter's breath, even though he has only just walked off the pitch.

After a jubilant team bath with exultant teammates, young men letting the enormity of their achievement wash over them, it is upstairs for champagne in the boardroom. Jim's emotions cloud as he enters the wood paneled room. This should be the greatest moment of his life but these men won't pay him what he's worth. The jostling feelings make him loud and cheeky, especially as he downs the free hospitality at a rapid rate. Jock Stein and Willie Waddell are there to congratulate Scot Symon. Baxter has read about their trip to visit Herrera. He saunters up to the pair. "Hey, Mister Waddell, Mister Stein, you could ha'e saved yerselves the airfare and come an' learnt from me!" "A great victory" Waddell concedes. "We'll see who learns from who on Saturday." Stein says with a smile but hard eyes, referring to the Scottish Cup tie that Rangers must play against Hibs in three days' time. Everyone knows it will be Stein's last game in charge of the Edinburgh team before he moves to become manager of his beloved Celtic. "Aye, see you then." Baxter replies as he waltzes off.

Chairman Lawrence shakes Jim's hand and tells him "Well done". It is more than Jim can bear and he decides to head into the town but remembering the plan to sell him once Rangers lose in Europe, he begins to sing, loud enough for Lawrence to hear. "I'm no awa tae bide awa, I'll aye be back to see ye!"

Chapter 8

I'll send you twa tickets
tae the final, Billy!

March to May 1965

I n 1965 Scotland had a number of supremely skillful players, many of whom drank too much. One of them was Willie Hamilton of Hibs. Jock Stein's arrival at Easter Road had rejuvenated his career. In a 1964 friendly with Real Madrid, Hamilton had outshone the Spanish masters as Hibs won 2-0. Now on 6th March 1965 it was Stein's last game in charge of Hibs. His players wanted to give him a send-off, Hamilton wanted Stein to take him with him to Celtic. Hibs had class throughout their team. Stanton and Cormack the young guns in midfield, strong Neil Martin up front. Rangers played like Wednesday's epic victory had taken a lot out of them and if Jim Baxter played like he had been celebrating from Wednesday night to Saturday morning, it was because he had.

Hibs won 2-1, with Hamilton scoring both. Rangers were 5th in the league with no realistic chance of catching Kilmarnock and Hearts at the top. Their domestic season effectively ended with the Hibs cup defeat. All that was left was Europe and the small matter of the European Cup semi-final. Frustratingly for Rangers, their opponents were not yet known. German champions Cologne and English champions Liverpool had fought out two tough 0-0 draws, with both teams still in their domestic cup competitions, their play-off had been put off until 24th March. There were also international matches scheduled for April and May. It meant that

Rangers' semi-final against either Cologne or Liverpool might be weeks after Rangers' domestic season ended. In the other semi-final Benfica had drawn the team everyone had wanted out of the last four, Hungarian surprise packages Vasas Gyor.

Bill Shankly's Liverpool were also focused on becoming the first British team to win the European Cup. In a hectic week in late March they secured a place in the FA Cup final through beating Chelsea 2-0 and three days before that in Rotterdam they played out 120 minutes against Cologne with the score tied at 2-2. There were no penalty shoot outs, so straight after the final whistle the referee calls the two captains to the centre circle. Big Ron Yeats calls tails, the coin spins and falls and hits a divot balancing on its side. The coin looks like it may topple towards heads and Yeats suggests to the ref that he needs to spin the coin again. Just before gravity plays its part in football destiny, the referee retrieves the coin and spins it again. It lands indisputably on tails and Liverpool are through. The referee points at the anxious group of Liverpool players and Yeats raises his arms telling his teammates they are through. The Germans slump in dejection, at this cruelest elimination of all. Bill Shankly walks up to Yeats and asks, "Whit did ye choose son?" "Tails" Yeats replies. "Well done. That's what I would have chosen too." Shankly growls.

It is Liverpool versus Rangers for a place in the European Cup Final. England versus Scotland. The Ayrshire miner Shankly versus the Fife miner Baxter. It is also Jim Baxter, Rangers' left half, versus Liverpool's left half, Billy Stevenson. Stevenson and Baxter were born within a month of each other. Stevenson was living the dream at Ibrox, breaking into the team as a 19 year old in 1958, playing 26 league games as the title is won. The next season Billy Stevenson plays 60 games in all competitions, every single game except one league cup section match. He helps Rangers reach the European Cup semi-final and the final of the Scottish Cup. 23rd April 1960 ought to be Stevenson's happiest day of the season as the Scottish Cup is won, except it is the worst. Newspapers break the story that Scot Symon has got his man, the left half he believes will lift his side to a different level. Jim Baxter.

Baxter remembers Stevenson too. From an Under 23 call up in December 1958. Rab, Agg and Jim scrape together what money they can for Jim to buy a green suit from a tailor in Cowdenbeath. Baxter arrives at the Scotland camp feeling like a yokel from the countryside. No-one knows who he is. The Glasgow boys and Edinburgh lads, Billy Stevenson and Alec Young are dressed in the sharpest modern mohair suits. Stevenson is especially dapper. Baxter vows never to be upstaged in sartorial stakes again.

Billy Stevenson plays only a handful of games in Baxter's first two seasons at Ibrox. He is too young to be kicking his heels and emigrates to Australia in June 62. Bill Shankly remembers him and brings him to newly promoted Liverpool. He joins a Scottish colony with Tommy Lawrence in goal, Ron Yeats at centre-half and Ian St John at centre forward. Stevenson gets a second chance at football and in 1963-64 is part of the Liverpool team which wins the league. Now they are pursuing a place in the European Cup final and who should be standing in Stevenson's way? Jim bloody Baxter.

As Rangers league season peters out in a series of games with nothing at stake except a place in the semi-final team, 10th April should have been just the big match lift that Jim Baxter needs. England v Scotland at Wembley. Unbeaten against the Auld Enemy in the three matches since Baxter came into the team, this game he would lead his country out as captain. England, not needing to qualify for their home World Cup, are using their games to find the best squad and team formation. Both countries field strong teams, England with seven players who would play in the World Cup Final a year later. Banks, Cohen, Wilson, Stiles, Charlton .J, Moore, B. Charlton, supplemented by Thompson of Liverpool, Bridges of Chelsea, Byrne of West Ham and Jimmy Greaves. Scotland : Brown (Spurs) Hamilton (Dundee) McCreadie (Chelsea) Greig (Rangers) McNeil (Celtic) Baxter(Rangers, Captain) Henderson (Rangers) Crerand (Man Utd) St John (Liverpool) Law

(Man Utd) and Wilson (Rangers). Baxter and St John exchange a handshake on meeting up with the squad, "See you in May" they agree. St John also thanks the Rangers lads for seeing off Inter. "I didn't fancy meeting them" he confides. "And ye dae us? We'll soon see about that." Is Baxter's defiant retort.

The Scots' day out at Wembley is a typically colourful affair, full of tartan clad fans who have saved all year for the journey. The match is end to end but England take their chances. Charlton rifles in from 20 yards. Bridges passes to Greaves on the edge of the box and the ace goalscorer sweeps the ball home with a first time shot. Five minutes later Scotland pull a goal back Denis Law shoots from 25 yards and a deflection off Jack Charlton deceives Banks. England go down to 10 men at the stroke of halftime when Wilson hurts himself clattering into Willie Henderson. Byrne is also injured tackling Henderson and leaves the field for 15 minutes treatment. Scotland swarm over the 9 men. England are passing back to Banks whenever they can. Finally on the hour mark, Baxter feeds Henderson, wee Willie skips past Cohen and crosses for Davy Wilson to head for goal. Banks scoops the ball off the line and Ian St John is first to pounce to head the ball home for the equalizer.

Baxter is raging. Shouting at his teammates to finish the English while they have 9, then 10 men when Byrne returns. He wants to keep his record of always beating England. Scotland come forward in wave after wave but find Banks is in excellent form. The match ends 2-2.

The truth is that Baxter's head isn't quite right. He has asked Scot Symon if winning the European Cup would be grounds for a raise. Symon replies that there will be a one-off bonus but no change to the Ibrox wage structure. Baxter is torn. He knows he has to leave but doesn't want to. For once he is not sure that he wants to be in the shop window.

His sense of disquiet is heightened by the furious reaction of the Scottish Press to the 2-2 comeback against England at Wembley.

"Wembley Wasters-Scotland's day of shame" screams the Daily Record. "The atmosphere here is more funereal than four years ago" states the Sunday Post, remembering the 9-3 defeat. The Daily Express asks, "Are Jim Baxter and Denis Law expensive, temperamental luxuries that Scotland can no longer afford? Baxter can hardly call himself a great captain when he cannot even lead his side to victory over 9 men."

Across Glasgow, in the SFA headquarters at Park Gardens and at Celtic Park, changes are taking place that will have a profound impact on Jim Baxter and Scottish football. SFA chairman Willie Allan convenes a secret meeting that agrees to give manager Ian McColl one more match to show he is the man to lead Scotland to the World Cup. They do not tell McColl. Meanwhile at Celtic Park, the Jock Stein era has begun. Robert Kelly, the Celtic Chairman had hesitated at appointing the club's first Protestant manager. At first, he asked Jock to be assistant to Sean Fallon, then co-manager, then he listened as Jock explained he would only come if he was given Herrera level control. Signings, team selection, training and tactics. Celtic have not won the League or Cup since 1954 when Stein himself was captain, Kelly grants Jock Stein his Herrera deal and within three months the Scottish Cup is won, Dunfermline beaten 3-2 is a close fought final. The victory gives Stein the start he needs to relax into control of the club. It also brings Celtic the guarantee of European football for next season, something Rangers can only achieve if they win this season's European Cup.

24th April the Scottish League season finishes on an extraordinary final Saturday and neither of the Old Firm are involved. Hearts start the day two points ahead of Kilmarnock with the two sides playing at Tynecastle. The complicated rules of goal average mean that Kilmarnock must win by at least two goals. Manager Willie Waddell urges his players to remember the night earlier in the season when they came back from a 3-0 first leg deficit to beat Eintracht Frankfurt 5-1. Kilmarnock achieve the 2-0 win. Remembering the Herrera lesson of tight defence, Waddell's team have conceded only 33 goals in a 34 match season. Hearts have scored almost 30 goals more but goal average favours defensive football and Kilmarnock are champions according to the rules in force on the day. Rangers finish 5th and Celtic 8th. The 13 league games Celtic have lost that season are more than they will lose in the rest of the 1960s.

On 28th April Jim Baxter travels to the English Midlands to play in the Stanley Matthews' Testimonial. It is, in truth, more of a chance to mix with the great and the brilliant of the last twenty years of football. German fullback Karl Heinz Schnellinger does not exactly go in hard on the 50 year old Matthews on his big night. Call offs to Stan's English League XI, caused by Manchester United playing to win the league and West Ham playing for a place in the European Cup Winners Cup Final, result in Baxter switching from the World XI to Stan's team. It does allow Jim to slip through Jimmy Greaves to score past Yashin, in a glimpse of what might have been had Tottenham taken a gamble on the Scotland star. 35,000 fill Stoke's Victoria ground and 112 million around the world watch on television or listen in on radios as the World XI win 6-4 with goals from Puskas 2, Masopust, Kubala, Van Den Boer and Jim's clubmate, Willie Henderson. Bryan Douglas 2, Greaves and the only uncapped player on the pitch, Stoke's John Ritchie, score for Stan's team. It is a taste of English football for Baxter, both to prepare for the Liverpool game in 7 days and to sample it for the future. Baxter plays in red and white stripes.

Jim is thinking of the future in more ways than one. His wedding to Jean is only one month away. His father-in-law offers to buy them a house. Jim bristles and rejects the idea. He wants to buy his wife a house from his own earnings. It makes him more determined to take a stand against Rangers' antiquated wage structure. "Ye cannae keep a wife on Tradition and playing for the jersey" he tells himself. In his heart he still doesn't want to leave.

On 1st May Liverpool play another grueling 120 minutes to beat Leeds 2-1 after extra time in the FA Cup Final. Ian St John leaps in front of Gary Sprake to head the winner. Which team will be best prepared for the Battle of Britain scheduled for Anfield on Wednesday? Liverpool, tired but elated, inspired by the words of maverick genius, Bill Shankly or Rangers, rested but listless, with a captain who doesn't know if he wants to play for a board who no longer want him?

• •

Liverpool versus Rangers for a place in the European Cup Final. Two port cities, two British footballing giants. A capacity crowd of 60,000 packed into Anfield 40,000 red, 20,000 blue. The cauldron has been stoked further on Sunday 2nd May when Liverpool parade through packed streets with the FA Cup. Shankly two arms outstretched like an emperor in front of adoring legions. Anfield with its fans so close to the pitch is a cockpit of noise and emotion. Shankly has told his players exactly what to expect. Rangers, for all the words of Scot Symon and Jim Baxter in the dressing room, look stunned when they enter the park.

Three minutes in and Geoff Strong releases Ian Callaghan. The winger outpaces Caldow and puts in a perfect cross for Roger Hunt to volley home. Rangers are shocked but to their credit they begin to find their rhythm and come back. The game is not so much end to end as wave to wave. Ten minutes on the clock and Baxter robs Ronnie Yeats, who is trying to turn inside him instead of hoofing the ball up the park. Jim swings the ball to the back post where the smallest player on the park, Willie Henderson heads home. Now it is Henderson's turn to have his two arms outstretched as he runs toward his teammates in a hopping jig, face beaming with delight and incredulity.

Both teams have chances, the tackles fly in. Everyone has forgotten this is a European match, this is a good old fashioned British game. Yet it is a piece of practiced skill and teamwork that breaks the deadlock on 40 minutes. Straight from Liverpool's Melwood training ground. Peter Thompson is fouled by John Greig twenty yards out. Stevenson and Callaghan both stand over the ball as if deciding who is going to take it. Callaghan rushes up but jumps over the ball and continues past the Rangers' defence.

Meanwhile Stevenson does not sling in a cross but instead passes to Hunt who makes an angled pass to Callaghan, who slots the ball home.

"The next goal could be crucial" Scot Symon tells his team at half time. It is a pointless piece of advice. It is not as if his team could be trying any harder. It is not as if footballers don't know. Both sides hit the bar, McLean for Rangers, Lawler for Liverpool then on 75 minutes, Hunt fires in a shot that Ritchie can only parry and St John slides in to give Liverpool a 3-1 lead. The match ends on that score.

Jack Harkness of the Sunday Post writes "Rangers have spent all season perfecting a "European" game, on Wednesday night they threw it all away reverting to the good old fashioned cavalry charge of a British game."

Jim Baxter, always confident, is more upbeat. He swaps words with Billy Stevenson at the end of the match. There is more than a hint of their rivalry in the exchange. "We did you there, eh Jim?" Stevenson says, as the pair are walking off the park.

"Nah," replies Baxter, "it's only half-time. I'll send you twa tickets for the final, Billy!"

• •

Remarkably Rangers allow their selected players to play for Scotland in an international friendly with Spain on 8th May. The club's decision had been made when they became concerned at the 11 day gap between the end of the season and the first leg. They also noted that the match was in Glasgow, creating no inconvenience for the players involved. Greig, Baxter and Henderson duly turn up for manager McColl. Liverpool withdraw St John.

Jim Baxter continues to brood over a possible transfer. In the changing room before the match he asks the Anglos in the room if they have heard of any interest from their clubs. Billy Bremner, making his debut shrugs his shoulders. Bill Brown and Alan Gilzean of Spurs, glance at each other. "Dave put in a word for you." Gilzean starts, referring to teammate MacKay. "But Bill Nic was put off by your off-field reputation." Bill Brown completes the sentence. He sees the flicker of rejection in Baxter's face. "No offence, Jim. I'm just telling it the way it is."

Eddie McCreadie sees that the truth is now out in the open. "I'd love tae have ye at Chelsea, Jim but Tommy Docherty said "Two words: leopards and spots""

Despite all his overt confidence, Baxter feels his shoulders slump. Worse than that, a churn of fear in his stomach. He fights back in the way he does best with defiant humour, "And whit about you Yogi, any interest fae big Jock!?"

Celtic's John Hughes almost stumbles and falls as he is pulling on his shorts before a look at Baxter's smile shows that he is winding him up.

"You'll just hae tae stay with us then" pipes up Baxter's great friend Willie Henderson. "That's no so bad, is it?" adds John Greig. Neither Ranger wants Baxter to leave.

The match itself is a bad tempered affair. John Greig comes closest to scoring but Iribar makes a spectacular save. Zoco of Real Madrid is sent off for a foul on Law a minute before half time. The Spaniards leave the field at the end of the half, surrounding the referee jostling and gesticulating at him to also send off Law. Scotland can't break down the Spanish defence in the second half. The Rangers trio find themselves wishing not to be injured before Wednesday's second leg. In the last minute of the game, Reija of Real Zaragoza, is also ordered off for a foul on Bremner.

It is the second draw in a row where the Scots have faced, albeit briefly, nine men. The bullying Scottish Press go into a frenzy of criticism. "Shame on you Scots: I'm Disgusted" screams the Daily Express. "Scotland and Spain in sad spectacle" laments the Glasgow Herald. "The events of Saturday's international are more appropriate the subject of the pen of an obituary writer than a football reporter."

It is an obituary the Press are after. They are flexing their muscles to force the sacking of manager Ian McColl.
· ·

12th May 1965. Rangers v Liverpool. There is drama to come on the pitch and there are surely dramatic events being undertaken off it. In the crowd Scotland manager Ian McColl and trainer Walter McRae are watching the match with the double away World Cup fixtures against Poland and Finland in mind. A few seats away from them in the stand sits Willie Allan, SFA secretary and two seats beyond them Jock Stein and Robert Kelly, Celtic manager and chairman respectively. While McColl runs through in his head his team to play Poland, he does not realize that Mr Allan has already spoken to Stein and Kelly. When McColl returns to the Scotland training camp at Largs the next morning he will find out.

In Jim Baxter's breast rages the emotional turmoil of a lover who has taken the heartrending decision to leave because he believes his lover has betrayed him. Not valued his love enough. Will he ever find another who suits him so well? Who loves him so well? He knows his own value. He has to believe it will be so. 80,000 expectant fans inside the stadium. Baxter will lead out his team as captain. His last match at Ibrox.

It is another clash of the Titans. Lawrence and Ritchie both make smart saves from low drives. Forrest stabs a chance past the post. Jim Baxter is playing well, skipping past players with a shift of his shoulder, slipping through passes for diagonal runs but so are Smith, Yeats and Stevenson in the Liverpool half-back line. Shots are blocked. Time ticks on. Finally in the 65th minute a Baxter pass connects with a Forrest diagonal run and Rangers take a 1-0 lead. The crowd increase the volume as they seek the second goal that will force a play-off. 80 minutes and Willie Johnston appears to beat the offside trap to score. The linesman's flag is raised. The goal is disallowed. The Rangers players clamor round the referee Leo Horn of Holland. No goal remains the verdict.

Three minutes to go and Billy Stevenson tells Jim, "Guess it will be me sending you the tickets, Jim." Baxter's mind is clouded, he can't think of a humorously defiant reply, "Fuck off, Billy" he responds. In what feels like a fraction of a second later, the final whistle sounds. Baxter sinks to his knees. As the players leave the pitch Bill Shankly shakes the hands of every player on both sides and embraces Jim, "Hard luck, son" he says.

Dark clouds hang over the skies above Largs and Glasgow the next morning. Ian McColl takes a visit from Willie Allan who tells him he has lost the confidence of the committee and they would like him to resign. "But what about the last five years?" McColl asks. "It has all been about working toward this, the upcoming World Cup games. What has the last five years work been for?" "You have our thanks for everything you have done but you either resign with dignity or face the indignity of being sacked." Willie Allan replies. "The Poland match is only ten days away, one of our most important games…Who…?" McColl leaves the question unfinished. "You may leave such matters in our capable hands, Mister McColl" is Willie Allan's cold reply. Two hours later Willie Allan faces the Press with a prepared statement. "Mr Ian McColl has submitted his resignation as Scotland team manager. Consequently, he will not travel to Poland and Finland for the World Cup qualifying matches. Mr Jock Stein of Celtic has agreed to take over-but only for these two games. A decision as to the future will be taken by the SFA Selection Committee when it is appropriate."

Jim Baxter lies depressed and hungover in Jean's arms. He hears the announcement on the radio. McColl has always been good to him, trusted him in the Scotland team. Stein he is not so sure about. "His own man", Jim thinks as he sinks his head back into the pillow. "Aye, well, so am I".

Even in his befuddled state he is aware that the combination of two such strong characters may not necessarily be a good or easy thing. He also has no inkling that McColl's next move will have a profound impact on his own future.

****

Chapter 9

Stein's Sizzlers.

23rd May 1965.

Jock Stein seriously considers leaving Baxter out of the party to travel to Poland and Finland. He likes Baxter well enough as a player but not so much as an influence on the squad. Baxter is not a man to follow the manager's direction, to adhere to a curfew and perhaps not even to carry out a game plan. Yet Stein has seen with his own eyes Baxter dominate Europe's finest. The second leg against Inter remains fresh in the mind. "You need your world beaters if you want to beat the world." Stein thinks. "Ach, well, he's no going to be my captain." Big Billy McNeil, whose goal late in the game won Stein and Celtic the Scottish Cup just weeks before, Big Billy is a natural leader. "He'll be my extension on the park. Not Baxter."

Stein's negotiations with Willie Allan, prior to taking the Scotland job, were not dissimilar to his discussion with Robert Kelly earlier in the year. Control. Stein must have control. The selectors who have picked the side for decades must give way. They can still report on players down in England, God knows Stein can't be everywhere at once, but final say must be the manager's. Stein has talked the dual role over with Mr. Kelly. Celtic must come first. Try these two games and re-assess after that. Stein is glad to have the Scottish Cup win under his belt, ending the hoodoo of the trophyless years. Despite their dreadful league form, he is pleased with the squad he has, especially the younger players coming through. He has already supplemented the team by bringing Ronnie Simpson with him from Hibs and Bertie Auld, who scored two goals in the Cup Final, signed from Birmingham. All he needs is a goal scorer to put pressure on Chalmers and Hughes. He has his sights on Motherwell's Joe McBride. Jock eats, drinks and sleeps football. He can afford to spend this time with Scotland and prepare Celtic for the season to come.

Stein wastes no time pulling the necessary strings to obtain a visa to travel to Poland to watch the Poles play Bulgaria in a friendly. He returns from Krakow with the type of ball they will be using on the 23rd. He conducts a practice match under strict secrecy, not wanting prying eyes to note the tactics he is working on. Control. Stein strives to leave as little as possible to chance.

His squad is impacted by the British teams still in European competition. Rangers going out is a bonus, all their players are available to him but now none of Liverpool's are. Manchester United, with Law and Crerand, have a quarter-final to play against Strasbourg but they will be available just at the right time and back at their club before the semi-final. West Ham are due to play Munich 1860 in the Cup Winner's Cup Final but the Hammers have no Scottish players that Stein knows of.

Meanwhile Jim Baxter watches a phone that doesn't ring. No Manchester United, Spurs, Arsenal, Chelsea or Inter Milan. The headlines for the wrong reasons are weighing more heavily than those for the good. Rangers have made it clear there will be no wage increase. Baxter cannot face backing down and returning with his tail between his legs, after all that has been said. He should have the world at his feet, in his head he does but on 18th May he experiences the cold chill of doubt. What if no-one makes a bid for him?

The next day he is due to travel to Largs to join the Scotland squad. The day after, Law and Crerand will join the party after playing Strasbourg in the European Fairs Cup Quarter Final and the whole squad will fly to Poland. It is great to be keeping active with such important games, Baxter just wishes his future was more settled. A telegram arrives, Jim goes to the door with frantic expectation. He can't believe his eyes, it is from Billy Stevenson: "Congratulations on being in the Scotland squad-stop-do you still want two tickets to the final-stop-you will be playing Finland the same day-stop-will send if you can use them Billy-stop." The telegram boy asks if there is any reply.

"Fuck sake," Baxter smiles to himself. "Good old Billy." 27th May Liverpool play Benfica in the European Cup Final in the San Siro Stadium Milan. The same day that Scotland play Finland in the second of their World Cup qualifiers. Baxter thinks of the final, of walking out onto the pitch in the Stadium he has played in so recently. "Should have been me" he thinks to himself, as he remembers the disallowed goal in the semi-final, then he smiles to himself again, "ach, Billy probably thinks that about me being in the Scotland squad. He probably thinks that about my whole career!" "Good old Billy!" Baxter smiles again. He finds his natural optimism and confidence surging back after his moments of doubt. He runs through his mind whether there is anyone who might be able to travel to Milan at short notice. Maybe Cabrelli, the restaurant owner. "Nah," thinks Jim. "Billy has done his bit keeping his side of the on-pitch wager."

He asks the telegram boy to take down the reply, "Congratulations on being in the final-stop-Go on and win it for Britain-stop-can't use the tickets as I'm taking our country to the World Cup-stop-thanks for asking Jim-stop."

Baxter has no sooner paid the telegram boy and seen him on his way with the reply when the phone rings. "Jimmy, it's Ian McColl. I've just taken over as manager of Sunderland in the English First Division. I'd like to make you my first signing. To build my team around you. Like I did at Scotland. It's a great club, Jimmy, bags of ambition, good young players. I've money for more signings too. Your chance to show them what you can do in England. Close to the border, so you and Jean can easily keep in touch with friends and family. You'd be King there, Jimmy. King of Roker Park. I've already spoken to Rangers and they're happy to let you go. What d'you say, Jimmy? Jimmy?"

Baxter holds the phone away from his ear. After all the emotional drain, someone who wants him, who knows him and still wants him. Someone he's shared great days with. Rangers are happy to let him go. Bastards. After all I have done for them. All I have given them. Sunderland. Where the fuck is Sunderland? Don't know anyone who plays for Sunderland. Still, Mr McColl says I'll be King there. A chance to show England what I can dae, if they dinnae already ken! Fuck them.

"How much is the money? Will me and Jean get a house?" is all that Jim Baxter can think of saying in reply.

. . . .

"Fuck sake" Jim Baxter says, as do all his teammates, as they examine the straw mattresses, sharp metallic sprung beds, reminiscent of prison beds, in the Chorsow Hiking and Tourist Association hostel. "Hey, Jock, didn't the SFA tell them we were footballers, no political prisoners!?" Baxter shouts.

"Jesus, Paddy," he says to roommate Crerand, "we'll no pull ony burds in these!"

"Fuck sake, Jimmy," Crerand replies, "you're getting married in a month, remember?! I'm going tae you're wedding. No that I'm your best man, ya eejit!"

Baxter has not yet said a final yes to Sunderland but he has given Ian McColl a great deal of encouragement, including promising him that he is ready to settle down, about to get married, new club, fresh challenge, World Cup campaign to fight for; new Jim Baxter.

Jim can't quite forget that Sunderland is not the instant access to European football he was hoping for. On 23rd May he applies transference and asks his teammates, "Chorsow, where the fuck is Chorsow?"

Jock Stein believes he has already given his players all the explanation they could possibly need. Based on his observations of the game against Bulgaria he has explained how he believes

Poland will play and how Scotland, each Scotland player selected, should play, to best counter it. The changing room before the match, Stein hears Baxter's out of place outburst and decides to reply to it.

"Where the fuck is Chorsow? They fought the Nazis here for three days before the city fell. Their Jews and intellectuals were sent to concentration camps. Then, when they thought freedom was round the corner, the Red-fucking-Army took them tae be a part of the Soviet-fucking-Empire. There have been silver and coal miners here in Chorsow, since records began. Some of us ken what being a miner means, don't we Jim?" Stein stares hard into Baxter's face. Jim can only nod. "These are proud, hard people, same as we are proud, hard people. They may have put us up in a prison cell but that doesn't mean their footballers don't want to beat us more than anything else on earth. We need tae be at the top of our game. These two games before the season ends, I want three points, minimum, four if we can. No complacency, no fannying about, we treat these Poles with respect. If we get a draw, I'll no be unhappy."

Jock's words wash over the changing room. Some of the players know only Jock. John Hughes and Billy McNeil of Celtic, Neil Martin of Hibs, winning his first cap. Baxter just cannot let it lie, it is in his nature, it is who he is. The players are pulling up their socks, tying up their boots. "I hae all due respect for the miners o' Chorsow having been doon a pit masel," Baxter begins, "but consider this," he cannot stop himself, "I havenae heard of any of the Polish players. No even heard of their clubs. Odra Oploe, their skipper plays for. Polonia Bryton, Zaglebie Sosnowlec. I mean no disrespect, Mr. Stein, but, fuck sake, how are we supposed tae compare ourselves, except in European competition. I haven't heard of any of these clubs in European semi-finals . Broony here, he's won a European medal. Hammy, he reached a European Cup semi-final." " Aye, and we were cheated" the usually chirpy Alec Hamilton replies, " Me, Greigy, and wee Wullie, we were a' in a European Cup Semi-Final as ye a' ken. Me, I've played in a Final. Denis and Paddy, they're about tae play in a Semi-Final. We are better than them. I ken it. We can beat these."

Jock Stein rankles at the insubordination but he listens to the truth of the words and decides to let them be. "I said four points if we can, and four points I fuckin' mean. The players who haven't been to European Semis is only because their time has no' yet come," Stein says, looking at Billy McNeil, as if handing him a warrior's sword. "Go out there and win your country two fucking points!"

• •

The teams go out to play in a torrential downpour, "It's no as if ye've never played in rain before," Stein tells his players, as they take to the park. Nobody scores in a bedraggled first half, on 50 minutes Lentner of Gornik Zabre scores. Scotland launch wave after wave in search of the equalizer.

Denis Law, who has been playing in a deeper role behind Neil Martin, moves to centre forward, Martin moves to the left wing. Straightaway, Law leaps high to head a Henderson cross toward goal. Szymkowiak, the keeper, can only touch it onto the post, Martin stabs the rebound inches wide. 75 minutes, Scotland are no longer to be denied, Law fires home from the edge of the box. "Now," thinks Jim, "we push for a winner". Scotland are good but with Baxter, they are better.

Five minutes to play and Baxter chips Willie Henderson away. He reaches the ball, on the edge of the penalty box, before Gmoch of Legia Warsaw, shoves and kicks him onto the turf. Russian referee Alimov, aware of his duty to fellow Soviet bloc sides, waves play on.

"Fuck's sake" thinks Jim Baxter. A minute later he picks up a pass from Paddy Crerand and spins an identical ball, like a golfer playing a sand wedge, onto the path of Willie Henderson. Gmoch clatters into him, exactly like before. This time, referee Alimov weighs his reputation and future in the game higher than his obligation to the new world order. Alimov points to the spot. Jim Baxter picks up the ball. For a moment, Denis Law, Jock's designated penalty taker, looks to dispute who should take it, "I fuckin' won it, Denis." Baxter smiles, as he takes the ball from his friend.

Second penalty of his international career. Far more important than England 1963, Baxter puts Scotland 2-1 in front. It is a lead they hold until the final whistle. It is a lead that puts fear and doubt into the minds of group rivals Italy, who one month earlier had only managed a draw in Chorsow.

The Newspapers are as positive about Stein's Scotland as they were negative about McColl's. "Stein's Sizzlers" is Hugh Taylor of the Daily Record's headline. Jock Stein tells the Daily Express, "This is a team game and our team did exactly the job I sent them out to do and did it with great spirit. I see great possibilities."

Chapter 10

What's there tae dae in Helsinki?!

27th May 1965

I t was always going to happen, it just happened a bit earlier than might have been expected.

Jim Baxter crosses Jock Stein and pays the price.

It starts amid the jubilant celebration of the victory over Poland. Stein corners Baxter and Law about the penalty. "What was that all about? I said Denis was to take the penalties." "But boss, I scored!" Baxter replies. "Thank your fucking stars that you did." Stein growls. "Next time you do as you're told, understand?" Stein waits for a response. After a pause both men mutter, "Yes, boss."

Then comes the lecture. "We will be three nights in Helsinki before the match. There will be light training everyday to keep us all in shape and in the evenings there will be no drunkenness and a strict midnight curfew. We will attend a reception at the British Consul. You are ambassadors for your country, here to finish the job and beat the Finns. There is no point beating Poland and messing up against Finland because some of you go out on the town in Helsinki."

Baxter whispers to Willie Hamilton. "Helsinki, what the fuck is there tae dae in Helsinki!?"

It comes to a head at 2am on the morning of the 26th. A merry Baxter taps on the ground floor window of his non-drinking roommate, Pat Crerand. Pat opens the window and Jim catches the worried expression on his friend's face as he tumbles into the room.

Jock Stein is sitting on Jim's bed. "Do you think I was fucking born yesterday!?" Stein thunders as he stands. "I gave everyone a clear warning. Explained what was expected. Get yourself to bed, Baxter, we'll speak in the morning."

10 am in a room borrowed from the Hotel manager, Stein tells Baxter he is dropped for the game. Willie Hamilton will take his place in the team. Baxter knows that Hamilton was out drinking with him until ten minutes to midnight but he keeps quiet about that. Stein shakes his head, "I don't understand it. Was it really worth it? You've let me down, you've let the team down. You've let your country down. I can't tolerate this from you. I won't. You might have got away with it with other managers but no with me. I don't want your excuses or explanations, just tell me that when you're sitting watching instead of playing, that you'll think about whether it was worth it."

"I will, boss, sorry." Baxter says, as he rises to leave. Stein tells him as he reaches for the door, "Think about it, son. The way you played against Poland, this team needs you but no at any price. I'll tell the Press it's tactical, so they don't crucify ye. Now get out!"

"Thanks, boss" Baxter replies as he leaves.

Scotland, without Baxter, stutter to a 2-1 win against a team who are mostly part-time. Denis Law misses a penalty. It is, however, six points out of six. Scotland lead the group by one point, with three big games to come in October, November and December. Poland at home and Italy home and away.

The same day Liverpool lose 2-1 to Benfica in Milan. St John scores for Liverpool, Simones and Eusebio for the Portuguese. Bill Shankly is bitterly critical of the Spanish referee, Ortiz de Mendibil. Bill tells Bob Paisley he is thinking of quitting football, "British players," he explains, "might put in a hard tackle but we play fair. The Latins dive, feign injury, hit you when the ref's not looking and when all that doesn't work, they bribe the bloody ref.

Ye cannae play against cheats." Paisley is the soothing influence to the emotionally volatile Shankly. "It's like boxing," Paisley says "there are some clubs in County Durham where you have to knock the opponent out to get a points decision. We'll just have to build a team good enough to knock the buggers out!" Shankly pats his friend on the shoulder, "Aye, Bob, we will!"

Chapter 11

As far as I can see.

August 1965

C harlie Hurley was born in Cork and raised in the east-end docklands of London during the Blitz. In 1957 he outplayed England's young rising star centre-forward, Tommy Taylor, as unfancied Ireland came within one minute of a shock World Cup qualifier victory over England. John Ayeto scored, a play-off avoided as England progressed to the Finals in Sweden. Hurley played over 400 games for Sunderland, helping them to promotion in 1963-64. He earned the right to be acclaimed by the fans as the "King of Roker Park"

"Nah, yer no. Move over Charlie. I'm the King of Roker Park now" announces Jim Baxter, in front of all Hurley's teammates. James Curran Baxter has arrived on Wearside.

Jim Baxter's rise to being one of world's top players is fueled by enormous self-confidence, that spills over, at times into arrogance. It only makes sense when he is helping teams win games of football. Many footballers hate losing, when the going gets tough they dig deeper for a result. Jim Baxter, on the other hand, loves winning, especially with a hint of humiliation for his opponents. When the going gets tough, Jim Baxter gets drinking.

Jim Baxter's game thrives on speedy skillful wingers, like Willie Henderson, Davy Wilson and Willie Johnston, who he can set flying with precision passing. He works well with intelligent forwards like Jim Forrest, Ralph Brand, Jimmy Millar, George McLean, who know when to expect a diagonal ball slipped through the defence. There is no-one better for Jim Baxter to play one-twos with, as defence is turned into attack, than the strong and skillful John Greig. Baxter has lost this cast of teammates with his move to Sunderland. He begins to regret having to play with lesser players. Worse than regret, he comes to resent it. His response is not to fight back but to lapse into an ever-increasing caricature of himself. By the time he moves to Nottingham Forest, two seasons later, the balance between natural fitness and the detrimental effect of too little training, too much drinking and eating has slipped decisively toward the negative side. By the time he moves to Nottingham Forest, he is not so much a footballer as a freak-show.

But in August 1965, this is all to come. Jim has not had the psychological fright from breaking his leg. The games for Scotland have kept him busy up to the end of May. He has stopped the traffic in Coatbridge as his wedding party passes through, he has a new wife, a new club and a football manager who has faith in him. Who has pinned his faith on him and with it their mutually conjoined hopes of succeeding at Sunderland Football Club. Baxter promises McColl he will rein the drinking in. He promises Jean he will behave. Sunderland are paying him the money that Rangers would not. Paying him what Baxter believes he is worth.

He also has his country to play for and his country is on the brink of qualification for the World Cup. A tournament to be played on their doorstep. Jim Baxter will only be 26 when the finals open at Wembley. This is the stage he is made for. The stage he believes he is made for. What greater incentive could any man have?

1965-66 the first leg of Jim Baxter's race against time. Can he keep the balance of his life on the positive side long enough to help Scotland in the World Cup?

Jock Stein is nobody's fool and this is exactly how he sees Baxter's situation.

August 1965 Celtic come to Roker Park to play Sunderland in a pre-season friendly. In Jim Baxter's 5 years at Rangers he lost only twice in 16 games against Celtic. That's how much of a big game player he was. That's how much he dominated Celtic and made them sick of the sight of him. On the park that is, off the park, Jim is utterly disinterested in the bigotry that blights the Glasgow game, remaining good friends with Pat Crerand and Billy McNeil.

Celtic beat Sunderland 5-0. Billy McNeil thinks, "Oh no, what's Jim done, coming here?"

Jock Stein sits down with Jim after the match. He has arranged for them to be alone.

"Jim, you know the Celtic board has agreed that I can stay on as Scotland manager as long as we are still in the World Cup?" "Aye, great news, Boss" Baxter chips in. "Well," Stein continues, "I want you to be part of my plans and because of that I think I have the right to speak with you honestly. As one miner to another, if you like. Jim, you drink too much, eat the wrong things, gamble and don't train hard enough. As far as I can see you are killing your career and possibly even killing yourself. That is none of my business. All I ask is that you slow down long enough to be at your best for Scotland for this coming year. One year, between now and July 1966. Slow down the drinking. I'm no daft, you'll no' stop altogether. Cut right back in the week before any Scotland game. The rest of your life is your own. Do you think you can do that for me, Jim?"

"I've never let Scotland down, Jock." Baxter replies, with more than a hint of steel in his reply. Stein breathes heavily, he is a calculator of men and he understands fine that Baxter has not vocalized assent.

"If you don't, Jim, I'll tell you, like I told ye before the Finland game. You'll not be selected and you'll miss out on the greatest chance of your career to play in a World Cup Finals. The stage your talents were meant tae be seen at. Not Sunderland. Jim Baxter of Scotland against the world's best at the World Cup Finals. You'd like that, wouldn't you, Jim?"

"You ken I would! Naebody but a dafty wouldn't and aye, if we get there, Jim Baxter of Scotland will show them. I can tell you that!"

"Good," says Stein, "then we understand each other."

• •

Chapter 12

The high-water mark.

Scotland v Poland

13th October 1965

Jim Baxter changes the way he lives his life for no man but he finds Jock Stein's words winding themselves round his brain. "The greatest chance of your career to play in the World Cup Finals and you may miss it". God knows he isn't likely to play in any big European ties with Sunderland, isn't likely to qualify for Europe at all. This now, October 1965, is his one big chance. The realization sours the taste of the Bacardi and coke in his hand. More often than before he finds himself pushing away a glass. He even hears himself saying, "Ach, that's me away hame, now lads." Not a complete change but enough to keep his body on the right side of the fitness battle. Jim is sitting in the "Venerable Bede" bar in Jarrow one Sunday afternoon, when he realizes, all the glory with Rangers, the big European games, the near miss against the Czechs in '61, the strutting round Wembley in '63, they were all leading up to this: his one big chance to grace the football world's greatest stage. Jim pushes his pint away and heads off home.

Of course, back in August, his instinctive reaction was to want to make Stein eat his words. "I'll show him," Baxter had thought, "I'll play so well Jock Stein will be begging me to play for Scotland." Except he doesn't. He can't. It is all so much harder for Jim. Players not on the same wavelength, tough games, every single week. There are good spells, great moments but not the same aura of dominance he enjoyed in Scotland. Sunderland are strong at home but dreadful away. A mid-table side. When the first international comes along, Sunderland are a respectable 8th in the league having won 5, drawn 2 and lost 3.

Scotland play Northern Ireland in Belfast on 2nd October. Stein selects Baxter to play alongside Dave MacKay, playing his first international for two years, following two leg breaks. Baxter's direct opponent is his Sunderland teammate, Martin Harvey. Captain for the Irish is Manchester City's Johnny Crossan, who has just left Sunderland and who tormented Baxter and Rangers in the 1962 European Cup for Standard Liege. Harvey plays well against Baxter. Gilzean scores twice for Scotland but Dougan and Crossan score for Northern Ireland, with Burnley's Willie Irvine scoring the winner for the Irish, with an overhead kick in the last minute.

For Jock Stein the football matches come thick and fast, as he juggles the dual role. He flies back from Belfast to lead Celtic into a League Cup semi-final with Hibs. No sooner is that match concluded then it is back to international action with the vital game against Poland at Hampden. Stein flirts with the idea of not playing Denis Law or Jim Baxter, who were criticized by some of the Press after the Northern Ireland game. He thinks back to the match against Poland in Chorsow and knows that he can't. More than that he decides to provide Jim with a speedy winger he knows well, eighteen year old Willie Johnston of Rangers. The team that lines up on 13th October is: Brown (Spurs) Hamilton (Dundee) McCreadie (Chelsea) Greig (Rangers) McNeil (Celtic, Captain) Baxter (Sunderland) Henderson (Rangers) Bremner (Leeds) Gilzean (Spurs) Law (Man Utd) Johnston (Rangers)

The Scots are roared on by 107,000 fans packed into Hampden. The highest ever Scottish attendance for a World Cup qualifier. Bremner's tigerish tackling is the perfect midfield balance to Jim's precision passing. Johnston has the beating of Szczepanski for pace. Gilzean comes into play with clever lay-offs and has an audacious back heel cleared off the line. On 14 minutes, Billy McNeil, now a potent attacking force at corners, stabs the ball home after Kornek, the Polish keeper fails to hold the ball. The Glasgow Herald describes the first 45 as the "Finest half of football ever played by a Scottish team." Baxter feels the joy of playing with his peers reenergizing his legs. John Greig still remembers the drummed in advice, "Give the ball to Jim" and Eddie McCreadie, at left back, soon catches on. Baxter sets McCreadie on the overlap and his cross is headed home by Law. Minutes later Willie Henderson is tumbled in the Polish box but once again the referee waves play on. However, in the last minute of the half, Baxter feeds Gilzean and runs in for the return pass. Gilzean, instead of passing, jinks inside his man and his hacked down in the process. Even Mr. Carlsson of Sweden cannot deny this penalty claim. Baxter and Law look at each other and with a smile Jim hands the ball to Denis. Law scores and Scotland go in at half-time 3-0 up. "No more than they deserved" writes the Daily Record.

Scotland cannot keep up their relentless pace in the second-half. The Poles swap fullbacks to better cope with Henderson and Johnston. Jim Baxter tires and Bremner gets involved in a couple of altercations that sees him lucky not be sent-off. The Poles begin to test Scotland's defence, Liberda scores in 84 minutes and three minutes later Sadek makes it 3-2. For three tense minutes before the final whistle the Scottish players know they have put themselves within a fraction of wasting a chance of a lifetime. In the final minute Jim Baxter picks up the ball on the edge of his own half and plays a ball with backspin like a rugby kick for touch, staying in play close to the Polish corner flag. Willie Johnston sticks out his backside to hold off Gmoch, until the blissful sound of the final whistle is heard.

· ·

Chapter 13

We hae mair class.

Scotland v Italy.

9th November 1965

I t is Jock Stein's job to dampen down the rising wave of expectation and emotion, among the players and among the nation. Two points from two games with Italy will see Scotland qualify for a World Cup on British soil. Two draws, or one win and a defeat will be enough. On the other hand, it is perfectly plausible to imagine the Italians drawing 0-0 with Scotland in Glasgow and beating Scotland in Naples. That scenario is believed in by the Italians. In that scenario, Scotland fail to qualify despite their perfect start and what country is better at snatching defeat from the jaws of victory than Scotland?

"Of course, I'm pleased. The players have been immense, and I cannot ask for anything more than to be heading into two matches with our main rivals, with our destiny in our own hands. But the matches ahead will be tough, very tough." Stein tells the Press.

It is in Scotland's favour that there is so little time for emotions to run out of control. Less than a month between the Poland game and Italy at home. For Jock Stein there is little time for anything except football, having to fit in 4 league games, a League Cup semi-final replay against Hibs and a possible Final against Rangers, if that replay is won and an away European tie against Aarhus in Denmark. It is an article of faith for big Jock that he treats each game with respect, so much so that on 23 October the League Cup is won with a 2-1 victory over Rangers, courtesy of two John Hughes penalties but he cannot help thinking about the Italians and qualification for the World Cup.

At Sunderland, Jim Baxter is still behaving himself, as much as he can, to not fall foul of Jock's spies and keep in contention for the team to face Italy. Football in England is still running at a 50/50 win/lose for Baxter. In between the Poland match and the Italians coming to Glasgow, Sunderland beat Notts Forest and Northampton at home, draw with Stoke away and lose away to Sheffield Wednesday, leaving them now 11th in the table. Disappointingly the club has gone out the League Cup to an Aston Villa inspired by Willie Hamilton, with the tie being played on the day Ian McColl released Baxter to play against Poland. McColl has not forgotten the call-off headaches of a Scotland boss. Nor has he forgotten that helping Scotland qualify for the World Cup was once his job and still his fervent dream.

Stein hears no outrageously bad reports about Baxter's drinking. He phones Jim to tell him not only is he in the team but in the absence of injured Billy McNeil, he will be captain. Captain of Scotland for their biggest game of the decade. "I willna let you down, boss" is Jim's reply.

The squad meet up and Stein hammers home the need for discipline, determined professionalism, not to get too excited and lose formation, to keep going until the final whistle because the Italians will be hard to break down. "Don't do anything daft but keep going for the win," he tells the players, "because, make no mistake, this match at home will be our best chance."

When the players are playing cards in the hotel the evening before, John Greig remembers Baxter's inspirational speech before the Poland game in Chorsow. "Well, Stanley," says Greig, using Baxter's Rangers nickname taken from the comedian, "what are you going to tell us before the Italy match? You can't speak about European winners' medals, as they have far more."

"Easy, John," says Baxter, leaning back in his chair, taking a long draw from his cheroot to create a pause, "we hae mair class. Man for man, starting wi' yours truly, mair class than them."

Even for such an important match, Stein is prepared to blood new players. With McNeil and McCreadie out, he moves John Greig to right back and gives debuts to Rangers skillful centre half, Ronnie McKinnon and Celtic's Bobby Murdoch at right half. At left back he decides not to give a debut to adventurous attacking Tommy Gemmell, preferring instead the more solid Davie Provan of Rangers. The midfield is completed by Billy Bremner, with Willie Henderson, Alan Gilzean and John Hughes up front, supplemented by Jock's former Hibee, Neil Martin, who has just moved to join Baxter at Sunderland. Bill Brown, despite having lost his Tottenham place to Pat Jennings, remains in goal.

In the changing room before the match Stein talks through one last time what he wants each player to do. He turns to Baxter, "Any final words, Captain?"

Jim has no smart reply. He stands and picks up a ball, "We a' ken whits at stake tonight. Let's do our talking on the park!"

Exiled to Sunderland, Baxter feels the hairs on the back of his neck stand up as he leads his country out in front of 100,000 fans. It isn't fear, it is a sense of belonging. A warrior entering an arena fit for his skills. In the tunnel, just before stepping out into the noise, Baxter looks across at the Italian captain, Sandro Salvadore and behind him Giacinto Facchetti. "We beat you last year, we will beat you again!" He calls out. It is unclear if Facchetti understands but the Scottish players do. Jim's nerveless confidence helps calm the players around him.

Scotland, in a vital World Cup Qualifier under the floodlights. The match is frantic, both teams skillful and athletic. Although the Italians will be happy with a 0-0 draw they break forward when they can and have the best of the chances. McKinnon has to head off his line and Bill Brown, playing with a limp after an early knock to the thigh, has to make several saves. Greig also has to clear off the line. As the minutes tick away, Scotland do not launch a cavalry charge but instead keep playing with the professionalism that Stein demanded of them. Baxter at the heart of many of the moves with his neat passing and shifts of balance to take the ball past his nearest opponent. Six minutes to go and Hughes fires a snapshot wide. The Italians are cool professionals, they can sense a job almost done, come away with a draw and beat Scotland in the hostile home atmosphere of Naples.

"Just keep playing. This is our best chance." Baxter mutters to himself. Two minutes to go. Baxter shows for the ball on the edge of the Scotland box. Brown rolls the ball to him. Baxter moves the ball up the park through a one-two with Bremner. John Greig is running past Baxter in support. Jim slips him the ball, John gives it back. Simple accurate passing. Baxter sees Greig is running into space on the edge of the Italian box. He rolls the ball back to Greig, who fires a low drive past Negri.

The Scots go wild. The beautiful enormity of the moment. The whole outfield team piles on top of Greig in celebration. The final two minutes are played out. Scotland have qualified for the World Cup! The fans chant for a lap of honour and the Scotland team returns, John Greig in a white Italian shirt hoisted up on the shoulders of Davie Provan and John Hughes.

Chapter 14

Taking nothing for granted

Excelsior Hotel, London.

January 6th, 1966.

S lowly it begins to sink in that both England and Scotland will compete in a World Cup Finals held in England. Harold Wilson's Cabinet holds a special session to discuss logistics. It is bad enough having 50,000 Scots invade London every second year. What is to be done with that number or more, permanently camped in England until their nation's interest in the tournament is over? The English authorities have not had a problem of that magnitude since Bonnie Prince Charlie and his Highland Army reached Derby in 1745.

The banter in the dressing rooms of every English First Division club is spiced up, as the obligatory quota of three Scots in every team, tells the English lads that the host nation "has nae chance". The matches are extra energized as every player with a real or imagined chance of being called up to their country's squad strives to attract the notice of Alf Ramsay or Jock Stein. Adding to Stein's options, every player in the Scottish First Division, save for a scattering of Scandinavians, is available for selection for Scotland.

Jock Stein has his first chance to test new players when Wales come to Hampden on 24th November. Debuts are given to skillful Charlie Cooke of Dundee, Rangers' goal-getter Jim Forrest and the keeper who helped Kilmarnock to last season's championship, with less than a goal a game conceded, Bobby Ferguson. Stein keeps the half-back line from the Italian game of Murdoch, McKinnon and Baxter, with Jim retaining the captain's armband. John Greig is kept as a rampaging right-back with Eddie McCreadie on the left. Rangers duo Henderson and Johnston are restored to the wings with Alan Gilzean supporting Forrest up front. Scotland win 4-1. In only his second international Bobby Murdoch scores twice, with Henderson scoring and John Greig lashing in another long range shot. The only worry from the night is that Jim Baxter reports a knock to his ankle which may rule him out of the final World Cup game with Italy.

The Italian team has been bitterly criticized by their Press for failing to qualify. With the accusation of being a disgrace to the Azzurri ringing in their ears, the Italian team has pride and revenge to play for. The Scotland team is beset by a deluge of call-offs, real knocks and some only a club doctor can see. Baxter and Law are ruled out. Jock Stein would love to come away from Italy with at least a draw to finish the campaign unbeaten. Adam Blacklaw of Burnley is named as keeper, with Provan, McCreadie, McKinnon and Ron Yeats of Liverpool in defence. Murdoch, Bremner and Greig in midfield with Cooke, Forrest and Hughes up front. Scotland lose 3-0, confirming just how important it was to not need a result in the away fixture with Italy to qualify.

January 1966 turns into a hectic dream month for Jock Stein. On 3rd January Celtic beat League rivals, Rangers 5-1 and later in the month they knock Dinamo Kiev out of the European Cup Winners Cup, winning 4-1 on aggregate. On 6th January, Stein and SFA secretary, Willie Allan, fly to London to attend the televised draw for the World Cup. Stein tells the waiting Press "Having beaten one of the favourites, Italy, we have no cause to fear any team. We'll take whatever the draw brings." Four groups of four, with two from each group going through to the knockout stages. Scotland are in pot three meaning there will be two teams rated higher than them in their group. For any team making it through the group stage, there are only three games between that team and being crowned World Champions.

England are pre-set as first seeds in group one to be played in London. Uruguay come out the second pot, France the third and Mexico the fourth. A tough group, dispelling any notion the draw may be fixed. Playing in the Midlands, West Germany are top seeds, followed by Argentina, Spain and Switzerland. Group three, in the North-west draws Brazil, the holders, as top seed, Portugal from pot two, Hungary from three and Bulgaria from four. Group four will be staged in the North-east, closest to the Scottish border, Ayresome Park, Middlesborough and Roker Park, Sunderland. Soviet Union from pot one, Chile from two, Scotland from pot three, North Korea from pot four.

Jock Stein cannot believe his eyes. He has to use all his enormous self-control to suppress a grin. To stop himself yelling, "Ya beauty!" Willie Allan leans over and says, "Taking nothing for granted but we could not have hoped for a better group." Stein's eyes are bulging, he can only nod, fearing if he opens his mouth, he will say what his mind is thinking. The worst team from each seeded pot and Scotland. The draw could not have been kinder.

Sir Stanley Rous proceeds to set out the timetable of games based on the draw just made. Scotland will play Chile at Roker Park on matchday three, 13th July. USSR on 16th July and North Korea on 19th.

"Good" thinks Stein, Korea are unknown but we will have two games to watch them play. If a microphone was placed next to Jock Stein at that moment, you would hear him purring.

When Stein does face the microphones of the world, he has recovered his down-playing control. "The Soviet Union will be very strong opponents, Chile also and we must remember that Scotland have never done well against South American sides. North Korea I know less well, we will try to get to see them before the tournament and failing that we will have two games to assess their style of play."

A journalist tries to draw Stein out. "Jock, are you pleased with the draw?" Stein answers like an exasperated teacher explaining to a pupil. "Look, every team in this draw is here on merit but we're here on merit too. We have a chance in this group, like the three other teams. All I'll say is that we are in with a chance too."

• •

Chapter 15

Just another game.

Scotland v England

2nd April 1966

J im Baxter watches the World Cup draw on television. He is not a superstitious man. The supernatural being he trusts in, for good or bad, is himself. Yet he has a sudden sense that this has all been set up by some hidden force, higher purpose, meant to be. Perhaps shunting him career down a blind alley at Sunderland is so that he can know the Roker Park pitch inside-out to be ready for Scotland's World Cup games due to be played there. The local fans will be on his side and they will be supplemented by thousands, tens of thousands of Scotland fans. "Hold on," he thinks, "Russia and North Korea are communist countries. They don't let their people out for fear they will run away and Chile, where is Chile? It's thousands of miles away, anyway. Christ," thinks Jim, "there will be handfuls of opposition fans at most. Scotland will be playing three home games. I will be playing three home games." Baxter has been nursing a glass of whisky, not taking a sip, while he lets this sequence of thoughts work themselves through. Then he takes a sip, well more than a sip, raises his glass and roars to the empty room, "We can win this!"

In the English First Division, Jim is not a supernatural being. He dominates some games but not enough. Sunderland go out the FA Cup in the first round. Their only target now is to avoid relegation. It is not an experience Jim has had since he played for Raith. The team have four away fixtures in February and pick up only one point at Sheffield United, they also lose at home to Leicester and slip into 17th place, just above the relegation zone.

Despite managing Celtic through three competitions, the league, the cup and the European Cup Winners Cup, where they are in with a chance of winning them all, Jock Stein takes time to watch out for his players in English football. He spots Jim's slump and gives him a call.

"Mr Stein, to what dae I owe the pleasure?" Baxter answers.

"You know fine." Stein replies. "Your side has no' been doing too well recently. You've no' been making them win games."

"There are eleven players in a team, no' just me." Baxter retorts.

"You never used to say that when you were winning at Rangers." Stein lets the truth of the words sink in. Baxter decides to stop running and hear what his country's manager has to say. "I dinna need anyone tae tell me that. Out wi' it Jock, what is it you're phoning to say?"

"First of all, it's Mr Stein or boss, I am your manager for Scotland games. Secondly you remember that talk we had after we beat you 5-0?"

"Aye, I remember."

"You did well for me, Jim, in the qualification games. You did well for Scotland but you can't let it slide now. I asked you for a year, no' half a year. Till July 1966. 30th July if you want to know the date of the final. Are you doing everything to be as ready as you can be for that final, Jim?"

"I can always turn it on for the big games, when the need arises..."

"No!" Stein barks down the phone, insisting Baxter stops his games, his half-truths. "Jim, did you play when Real Madrid beat you 6-0?" Jim replies "aye". "Did you play when Tottenham beat you 8-4?" "aye" "Did you play when we failed to beat the Czechs and missed out on World Cup '62?" "Aye but.." "No buts Jim, they beat us and reached the final. A final we could have been in.

You could have been in. I know you, Jim. The miner fae Hill o' Beith. I know you because I worked down the pits for ten years and met many likely lads like you. And afore you start, I know you are special and the others weren't Jim Baxter, weren't you but consider this, the world over, there are lads in Buenos Aires and Rio de Janeiro, Dusseldorf and Dagenham who know they are special, know they are their country's best. These lads are going to be fucking hard to beat. Anything you can do to give your game its best chance of beating them, start doing it now, Jim. Five fucking months, that's all I ask. You're acting like you're all sorry for yourself for moving to Sunderland. Wake up! You have a World Cup to play for. A manager to convince you're worth a place in the team. Being drunk for five months will not help your chances of selection nor your ability to play, if selected. Do you understand?"

"I'll be at my best, boss."

Stein sighs heavily. "Jim, why am I phoning you?"

"I dinna ken boss, because you need me in your team?"

"Exactly," Stein states forcefully, "next time you're holding a drink, remember this. I need you in my team but I need you sober and I need you as fit as you can be. Scotland needs you as fit as you can be. I have nothing else to say. Over the next 5 months, every time you hold a drink, remember what I have just said."

"I'll remember, boss but we we'll beat them even if I dinnae."

"No."

"No?"

"I'm not going off this phone until you say, you understand and you'll drink less because you know what is at stake."

Stein listens to the silence down the phone. He is compelled to speak again.

"We'll never have this conversation again, same as we'll never, both of us, never have such a great chance of doing well at the World Cup. Show me the respect of making your answer real."

Jim Baxter bows to no man. To nothing. This is too strong, too real. The chance of a lifetime. What he felt when he watched the draw. Something that is meant to be. "We may never get this chance again. I don't want to let it pass me by. I'll cut back on the drinking and get myself as fit as I can."

"Good lad. You know if we are to get to the final, we'll have to play six games in a month?"

"The way I like it, boss."
• •
Following Stein's phone call, Baxter does try harder in training and cuts back on drinking and smoking. Results on the park remain hard to come by for Sunderland, especially away from home. "Just as well I'll be playing my Scotland games at home!" Jim jokes. Baxter suspects that Neil Martin is sending reports back to his old Hibs boss, but he is not angry if he is, because it would be in a good cause, giving Jimmy Baxter the best chance to shine at a World Cup. Sunderland beat Spurs 2-0 at Roker on 26th March and Jim is confirmed in the Scotland squad to play England the following week. "Hey, Neilly" Baxter shouts to Martin at training, "tell Jock I take two sugars in my tea!"

Ramsey versus Stein, the two managers have a month of testing and jousting ahead of the real business of the World Cup in July.

16th March sees the annual fixture between the Scottish League and the English League at Newcastle. Both managers field teams that reveal some of their picks for the competition ahead and some fringe players being given a chance to force their way into contention. Springett, Reaney, Newton, Stiles, Charlton. J, Hunter, Ball, Greaves, Kaye, Eastham and Charlton. R line up for England. Ferguson, Greig, Gemmell, Stanton, McKinnon, Dave Smith (Aberdeen) , Jimmy Johnstone (Celtic) Andy Penman(Dundee) Willie Wallace(Hearts) Joe McBride (Celtic) and Hughes for Scotland. The Scots win 3-1 with goals coming from McBride 2 and Penman. Greaves scores against Scotland again.

For the full international, two weeks later, Stein keeps six of the side that won in Newcastle, Ferguson, Greig, Gemmell, McKinnon, Johnstone and Wallace, supplementing them with three big English based stars, Baxter, Bremner and Law. Bobby Murdoch and Willie Johnston also return. Although Billy McNeil is injured, Stein does not give the captaincy to Baxter, preferring instead John Greig, who is emerging as a leader for Scotland on the park. Stein is keen to see how his Celtic maestro Jinky Johnstone plays at international level and how he plays with Baxter. Baxter's game thrives on quick one-twos, whereas Jinky rarely gives the ball back quickly to anybody.

England are growing ever closer to the eleven that Ramsey will field in July: Banks, Cohen, Newton, Stiles, Charlton.J, Moore, Ball, Hunt, Charlton. R, Hurst and Connelly.

The Scotland v England match has always been called the highlight of the Scottish football supporters' year. Saving up to travel to Wembley or the shorter trip to Hampden. Scotland call England the Auld Enemy, whereas England appear to hardly notice Scotland at all. Jock Stein is very clear to the players before the match. "I know this is a big match, with 123,000 in the stadium but with what we have ahead of us, it's just another game. A warm up for the World Cup."

Scotland start poorly. Baxter is caught in possession a couple of times. On 18 minutes, Hunt and Ball combine to square the ball to Hurst in space and he angles the ball past Ferguson. Referee Faucheux of France gives a bizarre performance, denying four clear penalties in the game, which, for sake of balance, are two apiece. The first is when Willie Johnston cuts inside Stiles in the box, with Nobby trying to swap shirts early. Five minutes later, Scotland are carved open again and Hunt scores with another low shot into the opposite corner. Just before half-time Denis Law leaps and twists to head home a Willie Johnston corner. In the second half, the second denied penalty comes when Baxter loses the ball to Bobby Charlton who sends in a cross destined for Hurst, until McKinnon punches the ball away. Kenneth Wolstenholme, commentating, sees it but the referee doesn't. A minute later, a slick pass from Ball releases Hunt, who playing off the shoulder of the defender, takes his chance to place the ball in the opposite corner of the net. Scotland pull Bremner back into a more defensive role, moving Baxter up to link with the attack. The move helps spur an exciting last half hour. Jimmy Johnstone plays a one two with Denis Law, who fights off a challenge to direct the ball back. Johnstone drives the ball past Banks at his near post. Scotland press for an equalizer but in 73 minutes Bobby Charlton drives low and hard from 25 yards. Ferguson must be unsighted as he does not dive as the ball goes into the corner of his net for the fourth time.

In the last ten minutes, Bremner slides through Ball's legs on the edge of the box. He gets the ball and Alan Ball but the referee cannot think so as he awards a foul, however, not a penalty but an indirect free kick. On 82 minutes, Baxter chips a free kick to the far post where Jimmy Johnstone comes in to crash another near post shot into the roof of the net. Scotland pile on the pressure in the last five minutes, playing in the second half as they should have in the first. Johnstone is fouled by Newton outside the penalty area but secondly inside, as Jinky rides the foul and carries on into the box. The referee gives the free kick outside. Three minutes later Billy Bremner is fouled in the box by Newton. The commentator is sure it is a penalty. The referee puts the free kick outside the penalty area again. Willie Wallace fires the resultant cross toward goal only for Stiles to head off the line. Scotland and Baxter's four game unbeaten run against England is brought to an end in a game which could easily have been a 6 each draw. Kenneth Wolstenholme states it is a match that will never be forgotten but he is wrong, as it fades into obscurity with everything that follows that summer.

As it should do, in a country not obsessed with a game against one country.

• •

Chapter 16

The squad assembles.

April to May 1966.

Brian Glanville writes, "The climax of the British football season, in England and Scotland both, is sprinkled with World Cup gold dust. Schoolboys and more mature supporters throughout both countries gawp in awe during matches, knowing that 44 of the players they are watching will make up the squads of two of the most powerful teams in this summer's tournament. In the pubs and clubs across the land, arguments rage about whom these 44 should be."

Jim Baxter, stung by criticism of his first half performance against England, finally digs deeper into his recesses of determination and plays a great game on 11th April as Sunderland beat title favourites Liverpool 3-2 at Roker Park. Harvey and Martin equalize two goals by right back Chris Lawler and Baxter sweeps forward to net the winner. A week later he scores again as Chelsea are defeated 2-0.

Liverpool and Celtic play out a hectic April. Both are leading their respective leagues when they meet on 14th April in the semi-final of the European Cup Winner's Cup. Bobby Lennox scores to win the first leg 1-0 but 5 days later Liverpool with goals by Smith and Strong make the aggregate 2-1. For the second season in a row, a late Scottish goal against Liverpool is disallowed, this time Bobby Lennox for offside. Celtic are deeply aggrieved as the final is due to be played at Hampden. On 30th April a Roger Hunt double against Chelsea sees Liverpool confirmed as Champions for the 7th time, finishing 5 points ahead of Leeds and Burnley. Meanwhile up in Scotland, Celtic survive a 14 points from 7 games finish by Rangers to win the title. Celtic's first title in 12 years. They are two points above their Glasgow rivals, a defeat to Dundee United in mid-March proving Rangers undoing. Celtic and Rangers have smashed their way to the top of the division, Celtic scoring 106 goals and Rangers 91. It is a remarkable first full season in charge for Stein, even more remarkable when his Scotland duties are considered as well. On April 23rd Rangers and Celtic play out a drawn Scottish Cup Final, with Rangers winning the replay 1-0, four days later. Danish defender Kai Johansen's 70th minute strike denying Stein a domestic treble.

Sunderland wind up their league season with a 2-0 victory over F.A Cup finalists, Everton. Sunderland finish on 38 points in 13th place. Fourteen home wins out of 21 games, alongside one win away from home shows where their problems lie. Jim Baxter's concern about the strength of the squad is perhaps illustrated by him finishing joint top scorer in the league for Sunderland, with 8 goals, alongside fellow Scots, Neil Martin and George Mulhall. Jim laments that he can't rib any of his teammates about their chances in the forthcoming World Cup because none of Sunderland's English players are remotely near the England squad.

Everton come back from 2-0 down to win 3-2 against Sheffield Wednesday in the F.A Cup Final. 19 year old Scot, Jim McCalliog, scores for Wednesday. Jimmy Gabriel, Alex Scott and Alex Young are the Scottish players in the winning side.

Liverpool lose a European final for the second year in a row, beaten 2-1 by Borussia Dortmund. Roger Hunt scores for Liverpool, Siggi Held and Reinhart Libuda for the Germans.

Real Madrid return to European Cup winning ways with a 2-1 victory over Partizan Belgrade. The Yugoslavs had surprisingly defeated Manchester United in the semi-final. The result made even more surprising following United's 5-1 away victory over holders Benfica in the previous round. Matt Busby will have to wait to fulfil his dream of European Cup glory. Barcelona and Saragossa play an all-Spanish Fairs Cup Final with Barcelona winning 4-3 on aggregate. Leeds and Chelsea are knocked out in the semi-final, both losing play-offs after aggregate draws.

For many of the top players, a season of 60 plus games draws to a close.

• •

Sean Fallon and Neil Mochan, Jock Stein's assistants at Celtic, have no official position in the Scotland Team set-up. As the deadline day for naming World Cup squads of 22 looms, Jock appreciates their support. "Don't look at that!" Stein instructs but mischievous Mochan has known Stein since they were players together and he picks up the folder marked "Forwards+ Wingers" anyway.

"Ian St John (28) Alex Young (29) David Herd (32) Denis Law (26) Andy Lochhead (25) Alan Gilzean (27) Neil Martin (25) Jim Forrest (21) George McLean (23) Alex Ferguson (24) Willie Wallace (26) Steve Chalmers (30) John Hughes (23) Bobby Lennox (22) Joe McBride (28) Charlie Cooke (23) Willie Johnston (19) Willie Henderson (22) Davy Wilson (27) Jimmy Johnstone (21) Alex Scott (29) Willie Morgan (21) Jimmy Robertson (21)"

"That's a fine attacking squad you've got there, Jock. Not many defenders though and you'll need at least one keeper." Mochan jokes.

"All good players. All doing a job for their teams. I can only pick seven." Stein explains.

"Joe, Bobby, Stevie, Yogi and Jinky plus Gilzean and Law." Mochan says quickfire.

"Neilly, be serious."

"I am."

"May I?" Mochan asks as he picks up the next folder marked "Half backs, inside forwards"

"Bobby Collins (35) Billy Bremner (23) Pat Crerand (27) Billy Stevenson (26) Dave MacKay (31) George Graham (21) Jim Baxter (26) Davie Gibson (27) Willie Hamilton (28) John Greig (23) Pat Stanton (21) Peter Cormack (20) Dave Smith (23) Andy Penman (23) Bobby Murdoch (21) Bertie Auld (28)"

"How many?" Mochan asks. "Five" Stein replies.

"Bremner, Crerand, MacKay, Baxter and Murdoch. Poor Bertie." Mochan says "I'm saving John Greig as a defender."

"Might as well go the whole hog," says Stein, handing over a folder marked "Fullbacks and centre halves"

"Ron Yeats (28) Willie Bell (28) Jimmy Gabriel (25) Frank McLintock (26) Ian Ure (26) Eddie McCreadie (26) Bobby Moncur (21) Tommy Gemmell (22) Billy McNeil (26) John Clark (25) Ron McKinnon (25) Davie Provan (26) Jackie McGrory (24) Willie Callaghan (23) Roy Barry (23) Alec Hamilton (27)"

"Not so many to choose from. How many?" Mochan asks. "Seven" Stein replies.

"Hmm, I've brought back John Greig, plus Billy, Tam, McCreadie, McKinnon, Ron Yeats. We're short of fullbacks, so Alec Hamilton."

"Not a folder, just a page" says Stein, handing Mochan a sheet marked, "Goalkeepers"

"Tommy Lawrence (26) Adam Blacklaw (28) Bill Brown (34) Bobby Ferguson (21) Jim Cruickshank (25) Ronnie Simpson (35)"

"Ronnie? Auld faither? Be a guy auld age for a first cap." Mochan says.

"Do you know a safer pair of hands?" Stein replies.

"No," Mochan answers "Simpson, Brown and Lawrence. I wasn't impressed by Ferguson against England. I ken it's 3 goalies I've to choose, I can do the maths."

"Thanks, Neilly," Stein says, "now get out!"
• •

On 11th May Stein tries out his fringe players in a friendly against the part-timers of Holland. The decision is in part dictated by Leeds, Chelsea and Liverpool still being in European competition. The only English based player in a team of home based Scots, is Jim Baxter. Stein has come to believe Baxter's self-assessment that playing keeps him fit. Dave Smith, Aberdeen's cool under pressure left-half has earned the newspaper nickname of the "new Jim Baxter". Stein partners the two with Baxter playing inside left. Ferguson, Greig, Provan, Stanton, McKinnon, Smith, Henderson, Penman, Wallace, Baxter and Willie Johnston. The Scots don't play badly but they lack a clinical finisher and lose 3-0. With the squad of 22 to be announced on 15th May, Stein has had a reminder that the old guard may still be the best bet.

Jock Stein enjoys the unique position of being the first Scotland manager to select the team. Yet in an archaic clinging to power, he must attend Park Gardens on 15th May to announce and explain his chosen squad to the now defunct SFA Selection Committee. As new ground is being broken it is not clear what might happen if the Committee objects to one or more of Stein's choices. The most likely outcome is that Stein, a man of principal and control, would resign, regardless of the glittering prize of leading his country to the World Cup in two months time.

"Gentlemen," Stein explains, "I will set out my squad and give a few words of explanation for players with less established records. I will give the number of caps each player has attained to date. Goalkeepers: Lawrence (Liverpool) 1 cap, Brown (Spurs) 28 caps, Simpson (Celtic) 0 caps. Non travelling reserve, Ferguson (Kilmarnock)3 caps."

"I hear Spurs have released Bill Brown" Bob Thyne, one of the selectors covering the English game interjects.

"Aye but no-one objected when Bill kept a clean sheet against Italy in his last appearance just six months ago. I see him as third choice, excellent experienced cover and an old head to calm the squad. As will Ronnie Simpson be. Defenders, full backs and centre halves," Stein is running through the list briskly not wishing prolonged debate, "Hamilton (Dundee) 24 caps, McCreadie (Chelsea) 8 caps, Gemmell (Celtic) 1 cap, Greig (Rangers) 16 caps, McNeil (Celtic) 19 caps, McKinnon (Rangers) 5 caps, Yeats (Liverpool) 2 caps. Non travelling reserve McLintock (Arsenal) 4 caps"

The committee makes no comment, Stein moves on. "Half backs and Inside forwards: Baxter (Sunderland) 31 caps Bremner (Leeds) 4 caps Murdoch (Celtic) 4 caps MacKay (Spurs) 22 caps Hamilton (Aston Villa) 1 cap. Non travelling reserve Crerand (Manchester United) 16 caps."

Willie Allan feels the need to question, "Hamilton over Crerand? MacKay included, is he not injured?"

"Dave MacKay was injured in April but I have spoken with his manager Bill Nicholson and he assures me he is fit again. Willie Hamilton has had a strong first season in England, he is one of the most skillful two footed players I have worked with and faster than Crerand. Gentlemen, may I proceed?" Stein looks round the table, there are some glances but no clearly articulated objection. "Centre forwards and wingers: Law (Manchester United) 35 caps Gilzean (Spurs) 10 caps St John (Liverpool) 21 caps Henderson (Rangers) 21 caps Jimmy Johnstone (Celtic) 3 caps Willie Johnston (Rangers) 4 caps Lennox (Celtic) 0 caps. Non travelling reserve McBride (Celtic) 0 caps"

"No Davy Wilson," John Lawrence, the Rangers chairman states, "after all the excellent service he has given the national team?"

Stein sets his heavy gaze on Lawrence, "And after all the excellent service he has given Rangers he is no longer in your team either. This is about two months in the future, not two years in the past."

Willie Allan speaks again, "St John ahead of our younger goal getters, Forrest or McBride?"

"St John has won two English titles and a FA Cup in the last three seasons, appeared in two European finals. He has the strength and athleticism to do well against top opposition."

Willie Allan has been writing in a small notebook. "Mr. Stein, I cannot help but notice a cohort of untried Celticplayers, Simpson 0 caps, Gemmell 1 cap, Murdoch 4 caps, Johnstone 3 caps, Lennox 0 caps"

Stein sets his large hands upon the table, "Glasgow Celtic, may I remind you, are Champions of Scotland. Now Gentlemen, if there are no further questions, I will send the selection to FIFA and release the details to the Press."

• •

Chapter 17

World Champions.

Scotland v Brazil

25th June 1966

It is unusual for two teams both about to compete in the World Cup, to play each other in a warm-up match but Brazil requested a match with Scotland to acclimatize themselves to Britain, before Scotland's qualification was achieved. Both countries agree to keep the intriguing fixture, even though it is possible they may play each other in one month's time, most plausibly as winners of group 3 versus runner's up of group 4. Brazil have won the last two tournaments and are one of the favourites to win this time. Their star player, Pele, who was injured for much of the 1962 finals, is back in the team. "It's only Brazil!" Jim Baxter shouts to his teammates as they rise to leave the changing room.

Jock Stein is using the match to perform two tests. To test how some of the players with fewer caps rise to the occasion and to test how thoroughly the Scottish Press support his right as manager to make the decisions he thinks best for the team. Stein selects six Celtic players in the team. Simpson, Greig, Gemmell, Murdoch, McKinnon, McNeil, Johnstone, Bremner, Lennox, Baxter, Johnston.

Stein wants to see how young Bobby Lennox's pace and clinical finishing adapts to a more central role than he has played for his club. With only three central attackers in the squad, Stein wants to achieve greater cover. He continues with Greig at right back and tests McKinnon and McNeil as dual defenders. Bremner is detailed to man mark Pele. In a foretaste of the tournament to come, Bremner is tenacious in his tackling of the great star, so much so that at the end of the game Pele refuses to swap shirts with his marker. "Perhaps you want my shin guards instead" he says in his deep voiced faltering English, without a smile.

In the first minute, Baxter slides a pass through to Lennox, who runs off Bellini's shoulder to score with his first touch in international football. Scotland hold their own against the World Champions and Baxter regains all his touch and swagger, consigning his poor first half against England to yesterday's news. Servilio equalizes for Brazil in the first half and Gerson has a goal disallowed for an earlier foul. Scotland's defence deals well with the forward line of Jairzinho, Gerson and Pele, that will gain such fame in years to come.

"I looked to see how some of the younger players coped with such an occasion, against illustrious opponents and I have to say I am pleased with the result. Food for thought before our first game with Chile in two weeks time" Stein tells the Press. Scotland have no further warm-up matches. Stein gathers his squad firstly for a week in Largs and for the second week at the Northumbrian Piper Hotel in Gateshead with access to Newcastle United's training and playing facilities.

World Cup 1966 is upon us.

Chapter 18

Scotland v Chile.

Roker Park.

13th July 1966

After the Brazil game Jock Stein asks Willie Allan to give short term contracts, until Scotland's involvement in the World Cup is over, to his two assistants, Sean Fallon and Neil Mochan.

"I am worried, Mr. Stein, that such a development may be viewed as creating a Celtic enclave within the Scotland set-up, you already have six players in the squad."

"Mr. Allan, I will have twenty highly strung professional footballers with me for one week in Ayrshire, followed by one week in Northumberland, then for the first week of the tournament. If we progress from the group stage, as I am sure you hope we do, we will be together for a further week or two depending on how far we go. I am going to need, at short notice, people I know and trust to assist me."

"I'm still not sure. Surely there are others. Why did you say twenty players?"

"Twenty highly strung professionals plus Jimmy Johnstone and Jim Baxter, I am going to need eyes in the back of my head!"

"Oh, I see. Very well, Mr. Stein."

And so, Sligo born Sean Fallon becomes the first Irish coach of Scotland.

The Scotland squad gathers for the tournament on 1st July at the Seamill Hotel on the Ayrshire coast. The backroom staff consists of Fallon and Mochan from Celtic and Walter McCrae, an ex-Marine physical education instructor from Kilmarnock. Stein gathers the rich assembly of playing talent in a private function room and starts with the thought that is most troubling him.

"I am ashamed to say that what worries me most, as we embark on this World Cup campaign, is not how to beat the opposition, not what team to select nor what tactics to use. It is how can I stop a Scotland team from beating itself. Three weeks we will be together, from now to the end of the group stage. Four weeks, if we progress to the knockout stages. Only four weeks! Out of your whole lives and I am worried it may be blighted by excessive drinking and ill-discipline. That I will be forced to drop a player or players because they did not heed this warning and toe the line. I need not tell you, this is a chance of a lifetime. Four weeks. Four weeks we will never be granted again. I fully intend to return to club football at the end of this tournament and looking at the Celtic boys here in this squad you can tell why I'll have more than my hand's full!" A ripple of laughter breaks out as the Celtic players squirm in their seats. "So, I know this four weeks will be a unique opportunity for me. Days I will never see again and days I hope to remember for the rest of my life. For all the right reasons. You all know and I ken you do, that there are players who are sick in their hearts, back at home, for missing out on this chance to be here. Denis, your teammate Paddy Crerand. Jim, he is your friend as well. He was so unlucky to miss out. I am sure Paddy would give his right arm to be here. And so would all the men of Scotland! Embrace this chance of a lifetime. Enjoy it. Don't abuse your country, your fellow players or me by breaking the rules on drinking, on curfews on being fit for matches. Don't push me on this." Stein pauses as he looks into the eyes of the assembled players. He makes sure his gaze meets that of Law, MacKay, Willie Hamilton, Jimmy Johnstone and Jim Baxter. "Three weeks is all I ask. Four weeks if you play as I know you can. Neil, Sean and

Walter will explain exactly what is expected of you, with regard to drinking and curfews. Make the best use of these four weeks. This precious opportunity. Next time I speak to you it will be about Chile, USSR and North Korea and how we plan to beat them. Let us enjoy this once-in-a-lifetime chance to play in a World Cup and to make Scotland proud!"

As Stein hands over to Walter McCrae to spell out the drinking and time-keeping rules, Jim Baxter pipes up "It willnae be a chance of a lifetime. The winners come back tae the next tournament automatically as holders!"

July 1966 opens to bright sunshine throughout the United Kingdom. At Seamill the Scotland squad completes mostly light training involving lots of ball work. A competition to hit the bar most often from the 18-yard line is won by Jim Baxter with only one miss out of ten. The players swim in the pool, play golf, have card schools in the evening, listen to John Greig telling funny stories and watch Dave MacKay perform a juggling trick with a coin. Stein uses his connections with the BBC to set up a projector and have the squad watch a film of their draw with Brazil, the 4-3 defeat by England and the 1-0 win over Italy. As well as absorbing the lessons from these games, the players rib each other and cheer when the goals are scored. Howling "penalty!" three times for the decisions not given in the England game. Stein reminds the players that the opposition will be no pushovers. He obtains film of Chile's 2-1 victory over USSR in the quarterfinals of the last World Cup. "They finished in third place," he reminds his players. He obtains more recent film of USSR's 2-1 victory over Wales in May 1965, which went a long way to securing the Soviet's place in the Finals but for all his contacts, Stein cannot obtain any film of the North Koreans in action.

On 7th July, the last evening at Seamill before the squad relocates to North-East England, they are treated to comedians Rikki Fulton and Jack Milroy performing a special version of their comedy show, "Francie and Josie". The players are in stitches as Josie ends up in a hospital bed with a bad case of "World Cup Willie", a humorous play on the name of the tournament mascot. The only cure is a spicy condiment, "Baxter's chili relish." "Aye an' Chile will no relish playing against our Jim" Francie says as Baxter hoots with laughter and Denis Law slaps him on the back.

The squad relocates to the Northumbrian Piper Hotel. Jock Stein confides in Sean Fallon, "I think we've made it, Sean. We're through the period I feared the most. Once the tournament starts the matches will come so thick and fast, there willna be any time for nonsense."

On 9th July, two days before the opening match between England and Uruguay and four days before Scotland's first game versus Chile at Roker Park, the players are allowed to meet up with their wives and girlfriends to go shopping in Newcastle city centre. Baxter decides to meet up with Jean at their home in Sunderland instead.

10pm the agreed curfew time, everyone is back at the hotel except Jim Baxter. Stein orders all the players to get an early night, the storm clouds gathering on his forehead. At 11pm he checks on John Greig who is rooming with Baxter but there is still no sign. "I'm sure he's just stuck in traffic, boss" Greig pleads on behalf of his teammate. Stein's attention is drawn to the lights and crunching gravel of a taxi coming to a halt on the driveway, dropping its passenger 50 yards from the hotel. A weaving Baxter emerges from the car. "Go to bed, John." Stein instructs as he makes his way to the hotel front door. Sean Fallon meets Stein in the foyer. "Leave this to me, Sean." Stein says.

Stein catches Baxter as he is looking for his bedroom window. He hauls him into a small office near the front desk. "Sorry, boss. I was wi' Jean, my wife," says Baxter, clearly full of drink, "she's no well. She may be pregnant, boss, wi' our first bairn."

"And does your wife drink like a fuckin' fish when she's no well and pregnant!" Stein bellows in Baxter's face. "I wisnae born yesterday!" Stein pats Baxter almost tenderly on the shoulder, "I warned you, Jim. I asked you for a year and you gave it. Now, when I'm asking for four fucking weeks, you foul up two days before the fucking tournament starts. What's wrang wi' you, Jim?"

"I'm sorry, boss, I'm..."

"Naw, you were sorry in Helsinki. It's not good enough. No two grown men should be having this conversation twice. You're out of the team for the Chile match. At Roker Park damn you! We need every advantage we can get. Now the Chilean manager will look at the papers in the morning and think Scotland are a mess, with a manager who can't keep his own players under control. God damn you, Jim."

The two men are standing within feet of each other in the small office. Baxter looks up sheepishly, "Will that be all, boss?"

Stein grabs the front of Baxter's shirt. He is remembering a story from 1963, after Scotland lost to Norway, when a drunken Baxter told Ian McColl and Willie Allan that he didn't want to play for Scotland anymore, or more accurately "you can stick your team up your arse"

"Make it easy for me, Jim." Stein growls, "Tell me I can stick my team up my arse."

The two men glare at each other. Baxter bristling at the physical assault. His teeth grit as he wants to say the words. To show Stein that he can't get to him. That he will always do things his own way. Baxter lets his body go limp. "I'm sorry, boss. It won't happen again. I don't know what else to say."

"Get to bed, Jim. I'll sleep on it. You're out the first game, for sure. I'll tell you in the morning if you're still in the squad."

In the early hours, Sean Fallon tells Stein he has to send Baxter out the squad. "He can spend the rest of the tournament drinking to his heart's content, with whoever he was drinking with tonight" Fallon advises.

"No," says Stein, "how he played against Italy, Brazil, against

Poland. I don't want us to be without that but I swear," says Stein holding up his thumb and index finger, "I'm this fucking close."
• •

The 1966 World Cup opens at 7.30 in the evening of 11th July at Wembley Stadium, where the hosts play out a tough 0-0 draw with Uruguay. Until the final, this will be the only match that opens with the National Anthems of the two countries. A decision made by the UK Government to avoid the playing of the North Korean anthem, a country Britain was at war with only 12 years before and whose existence as a country is not recognized by the UK. Stein and the Scotland squad watch the match on their hotel television.

The next day provides ample food for thought for the watching Scots. Mochan, Fallon and McCrae watch on television as Brazil beat Bulgaria 2-0 with goals from Pele and Garincha. In Sheffield, West Germany send a warning to the world with a 5-0 win over Switzerland. Meanwhile the Scotland squad and manager Stein make the short journey to Ayresome Park, Middlesborough to see USSR see off the unknown men of North Korean 3-0, in front of a half empty stadium. The Koreans are small and skillful but appear to be no match for the hard, physical, disciplined Soviets.

Jim Baxter cuts a disconsolate, hunched figure in the stands. Sunderland is filling with Scots. All the BnBs for miles around, the student accommodation at Sunderland Technical College, homes thrown open for profit or kinship. His own parents, Rab and Agg are now staying with Jean at the Baxter home. Travelling south expecting to see their son play on the World stage. Travelling with their fierce protective pride. To be greeted only by the headline "Baxter Out". "Scotland will open their campaign against Chile tomorrow, without Roker Park star, Jim Baxter. Manager, Jock Stein, told a press conference today, "He has been omitted due to a disciplinary matter. It has been dealt with internally and that is the only comment I will make. Now ask me about who will be playing.""

Earlier in the day, Neil Mochan has been detailed by Stein to visit

Jean Baxter. She confirms that she has not been feeling well and suspects she may be in the early stages of pregnancy. On the evening of the 9th, Jim stayed with her until around 9pm, drinking only a few glasses of wine. It has been, as ever, a reluctance to come straight back, that has led to the curfew being broken. "One or two for the road. We've all been there," Mochan reports back, before he looks into the eyes of tee-total Stein," Well, most of us, Jock."

At half time at Ayresome Park, with the Soviets leading by two goals to nil, the Press pack spots the Scottish players. Photographers cluster disproportionately round Baxter, until Stein enlists the stewards to help usher them away. The next morning, even though the papers have pictures of actual football action from the Brazil, West Germany and Soviet games to show, many have the picture of Baxter in the stands. "Odd man out" the Daily Telegraph declares.

At lunchtime on the 13th, despite his own huge disappointment, Pat Crerand places a call to the Scotland team Hotel. He wishes Denis Law luck and next speaks to his long time friend, Jim Baxter, "For Christ sake, Jim, sort it out." Crerand urges.
• •
If, after the second breach of curfew within their player and manager relationship, Jock Stein had expelled Jim Baxter from the Scotland squad, Jim Baxter would, at the end of his life, look back upon it with great regret and complete acceptance of responsibility. That was how he dealt with his life. At 7.15pm on 13th July 1966 the regret is almost unbearable. Baxter thinks back to the feeling he had when the draw was made, the certainty that it was all meant to be. Why he had chosen Sunderland. To play for Scotland at the World Cup at his home ground. Now he was taking his seat in the stand alongside his friend Willie Henderson and the rest of the non-playing squad. Surrounded by 30,000 Scots who love him and 10,000 locals who do as well. The 310 Chileans and Soviets being perhaps the only abstainers. Baxter

has taken a call in the afternoon from his mother and father. They have been unflinchingly supportive as ever but he can't help detect the disappointment in their voices. Jim asks Jock Stein, if after the press attention the day before, he can watch the Scotland match on television. Stein looks hard into Baxter's face, "You are still part of this squad. If you no longer want to be, watch the match on television and do not come to support your teammates at Roker Park." Baxter joins his teammates on the bus. At 7.15pm some Sunderland fans break into a chorus of "There's only one Jim Baxter!" which is taken up by a fair number of the Scottish fans. Sheepishly, Jim rises to his feet and gives them a small wave. As he returns to his seat, he hears a harsh voice saying "Ya fuckin eejit, Baxter! Whit are ye playing at?" and he realizes the voice is inside his head.

Dave MacKay takes Baxter's place at left half. Simpson, Greig, McCreadie, Murdoch, McNeil, MacKay, Johnstone .J, Bremner, St.John, Law and Lennox being the Scotland side. Although he wears number 9, St. John, plays a little behind Denis Law and the two wingers, making him available to scrap for the ball in the middle of the park, alongside Murdoch, Bremner and MacKay. It is the role he has been playing for Liverpool. The Chileans play in red shirts and shorts. They are tough and skillful, though perhaps a bit better behaved than four years before, when they fought out the notorious Battle of Santiago against Italy. That is not to say that Eyzaguirre doesn't take the legs from Jimmy Johnstone the first time he goes past him.

The capacity crowd is for Scotland. As predicted, every game in this tournament feels like a home game for the Scots. Olivares saves low shots from Law and Lennox. Greig shoots over and St. John has a header cleared off the line by Figueroa with goalkeeper, Olivares beaten. Twenty minutes into the match, a rare Chilean counter-attack. Leonel Sanchez plays in Pedro Araya, who goes past McNeil as he slips. The crowd is silenced as Chile take a 1-0 lead. Stein bawls at the Scots to keep their composure. Just before half time St.John, who can never quite forget he wanted to be a champion boxer, clashes with Marcos after the Chilean trips him. Both players have their names written into the referee's book.

Chile lead 1-0 at half-time. Scotland's disastrous record of never having won a game in the World Cup finals appears to be haunting them still. Stein tells his players they have been the better side and that the goals will come. "We did not come all this way together to lose" are his last words as the players go back out.

47 minutes, Johnstone evades Eyzaguirre's swiping foot and for once releases the ball early to Bremner who fires home from the edge of the box. Scotland are level.

Now, Scotland's superior play and crowd advantage drives the team forward. Murdoch scrapes the bar with a twenty yard shot. On the hour, MacKay sends the ball along the line to Lennox, who outpaces Vilanueva. His cross to the back post is headed down by St. John for Law to get his right boot onto the ball before the lunging Figueroa. The crowd erupts. Scotland are in the lead.

Twenty minutes from the end, MacKay crashes into a 50/50 challenge with Prieto. Both players stay on the grass. It isn't a leg break but MacKay's knee begins to swell immediately, a recurrence of the injury that had cost the Spurs man the last month of the season. Stein joins Walter McCrae and Tom McNiven team physio on the park. Substitutes are not allowed. "Will you take an injection, Dave, to help you keep going?" Stein asks. MacKay nods his head and a hydro cortisone shot is sent into the joint. Prieto is back on his feet. "Can you play, Dave? See out the game?" Stein asks. MacKay nods again, face set with determination. "Go back alongside Billy, no forward runs. Sweep in when you can."

MacKay appears to be limping for the first few minutes after play is re-started but for the last fifteen minutes he looks to be moving more freely, making two timely interceptions as Chile press for an equalizer. Simpson saves well from Tobar and Greig makes a block on the six yard line, from an Araya shot. Scotland do not simply defend the closing period, Eyzaguirre finally earns a booking for cutting short a Johnstone run. Minutes from the end, St John stabs wide from a Bremner pass. When the final whistle blows, Billy McNeil and Dave MacKay embrace.

In the treatment room, after the match, Doctor Hillis pronounces that MacKay looks certain to be out of the next match, probably even more. MacKay sits up on the treatment table and tells Stein and Hillis, "At least I helped Scotland get one more point than we managed in the whole of Sweden '58". MacKay and goalkeeper Bill Brown being the only members of the squad who have been to a Finals before.

• •

Chapter 19

Bobby's defected

Scotland versus USSR.

16th July 1966.

Roker Park, Sunderland.

Scottish officials and fans are taking an extra interest in the North-west Group 3. The winners out of Brazil, Portugal, Hungary and Bulgaria will play the runners-up in Scotland's Group 4. The winners of Group 4 will play the runners-up in Group 3. Scotland's incentive to win Group 4 is to avoid a quarter final pairing with World Cup holders, Brazil. On the same night that Scotland get off to a winning start against Chile, Portugal beat Hungary in what is assumed to be the battle for second place in Group 3. Two days later, Stein and Fallon travel to Goodison Park to watch as Hungary shock the football world beating Brazil 3-1. Pele is not able to play having been injured against Bulgaria. There is a very real danger he will be kicked out the competition for a second Finals in a row. Now it is far from clear who will win or come second in Group 3.

Whoever wins Group 3, Scotland must remain focused on their own matches. "Whoever comes out in the top 2 in Group 3 will be a good side." Stein tells the Press.

On the morning of the 16th, Stein gathers his squad and is using a slide projector to run through the playing style of tonight's opponents, the Soviet Union. "The Soviets will be tough, well-organized opponents. The older players, such as Lev Yashin were in the side that won the European Championship in 1960 and many were in the team that were runners-up in '64. Their dangerman is Igor Chislenko, a direct winger, who can cut in from either right or left," Stein clicks the next slide that shows Chislenko.

ick to add title

"Whoa ho!" Jim Baxter exclaims, "Bobby's defected!" Chislenko's picture, from the sandy hair to the luggy ears is the image of Celtic's Lennox. "Stick one through your own net past Yashin tonight, Bobby!"

The players are all laughing. "Shurely there's shum mishtake, Mish Moneypenny" adds John Greig, impersonating fellow Edinburgh lad, Sean Connery.

Stein is happy the players are so relaxed but he has a serious point to make. "Very funny, lads. Chislenko is one of the reasons we have been working on the flat back four in training. Against England we played two traditional half-backs and Billy was left exposed to deal with Hunt and Hurst. Again against Chile, we were better set up to defend when Dave was forced to stay back. England have Bobby Moore wearing a half back jersey but concentrating on supporting his centre half. The same at Celtic with John Clark. Tonight, against the Soviets, I'm asking John to play that role, alongside Billy. It may limit his forward forays but the full backs, Tam and Eddie, will be better covered to go forward. It's going to be a tight game and we'll be best building from a strong defence. Jim, Billy, it will also give you more freedom to probe forward. Any questions?"

Dave MacKay and Bobby Murdoch are the players changing from the Chile match. MacKay has flown to London for treatment on his knee. Stein has spoken privately to his club-player Murdoch about missing this match. The Scots will line up: Simpson, Gemmell, McCreadie, Greig, McNeil, Baxter, Johnstone, Bremner, St John, Law and Lennox.

If the Scottish team is filled by young men raised in wartime to parents impacted by war, what a tale must the Soviet players have to tell? All eleven of them a miracle of survival, they come from every corner of the Soviet empire. Forwards Malafeev and Banishevski from Minsk and Baku, midfielder Jozsef Sabo from Kiev, defender Khurlsilava from Tiblisi. The rest of the team are Russians, left back Danilov of Zenit Leningrad and the remaining five split between the Moscow clubs, CSKA, Torpedo, Spartak and Dynamo. The Soviets will play with a fierce patriotism but also a little fear and conformity. All in the team know the story of the golden player of their generation, Eduard Streltsov of Mocow Torpedo, who was sentenced to 12 years in a gulag on charges widely believed to be trumped up, his real crime, "showing excessive decadent western cult of personality" and sporting, in 1957, a western "teddy boy" haircut. Such an example will concentrate a footballer's mind upon what is expected but is unlikely to generate the creative freedom expressed by Baxter, Johnstone or Law.

To better distinguish the teams for viewers on black and white television, Scotland agree to wear blue shorts. The other distinctive visual difference is the "CCCP" emblazoned across the Soviet players' red shirts. Television in the United Kingdom faces its own test on 16th July with England playing Mexico at Wembley the same night. The BBC runs with the England match, while STV covers the Scotland game.

As with the Chilean game, the Roker Park crowd is hugely pro-Scotland. Jim Baxter runs out onto the turf he knows so well and, this time, waves acknowledgement, without any guilt, to the roars of the crowd. The Sunderland fans in the stadium may have some misgivings that their new "king" did not reach the heights expected but they are happy enough with the 14 wins out of 21 games their side achieved at home. In any case, 35,000 out of the 40,000 crowd are Scottish, having either travelled down that day or part of the growing Scottish encampment in England's North-east. The Soviet players know they are in an away game.

The game itself develops into a physical, technical and tactical chess-match. McCreadie is tasked to follow Chislenko everywhere, including switching wings with Gemmell when Chislenko moves. John Greig controls his natural desire to pile forward, providing constant cover to McNeil in defence. In front of them, Bremner breaks up Soviet moves and Baxter is all neat, crisp passing, if not easily finding the killer penetrative ball, because Scotland are equally contained. Lennox and Johnstone struggle to evade Ponomarev and Danilov, Soviet captain, Shesterniev has the measure of Denis Law. There are a few shots from each side that fizz past the post or provide easy saves for the 36 year old veterans, Yashin and Simpson, in goal. Deadlock at 0-0 when the half-time whistle blows.

Just over a year ago the Scottish fans and Press had indulged in an orgy of criticism because their team drew 0-0 with Spain in a hard fought match at home. Now there is a sense that the Scottish audience is maturing. Their sights are not set on glory or an annual trip to Wembley, instead they understand that 0-0 may be just what is needed for the immediate job in hand of qualification within a tournament of international significance. The crowd stay supportive, encouraging the players to keep patient. To keep tight in defence and to keep probing away.

The game flares up in 70 minutes when St John, foraging ever deeper for the ball, is tripped heavily by Voronin. Colleagues rush to separate the players in ensuing pushing match, which sees both players noted into West German referee, Rudolf Kreitlein's book. A second booking of the tournament means St John will be unavailable for the next match.

The minutes tick away. The managers of each side know that Chile and North Korea have drawn 1-1 the night before. Three points for both Scotland and USSR from the first two games will see the final match in their own hands. Not to lose becomes the priority creeping through both teams' play.

Except no-one has told Jim Baxter. He takes a short pass from Greig on the halfway line. He drops his shoulder and goes round Sabo, releasing the ball, just before Voronin tackles him, to Law. Denis out-muscles Shesterniev to control the ball and direct it forward into the path of Baxter who has skipped over Voronin's attempted block and continued his run. Danilov coming across to cover, slides into Baxter's legs just after Jim has poked the ball an inch beyond the Soviet defender's reach. Penalty! The enormity of failing in their task so late in the game, combined with suspicions of western conspiracy to deny them, causes the normally disciplined Soviet players to crowd round the referee in heated protest. Mister Kreitlein waves them away.

Baxter picks himself up then picks up the ball. This time by manager's pre-agreement and pre-match practice. Baxter remembers playing with Yashin for the Rest of the World. Remembers the great Russian keeper praising him, in faltering English, for the penalty he scored against England in '63. Low to the goalkeeper's left. No time to dwell on it further. With nerveless efficiency Baxter curves the ball high to the keeper's right, with Yashin already moving the wrong way.

In the crush of congratulations, the guilt at missing the first game is washed away. "This is where I am meant to be," Jim thinks, "an' I'm no going tae make a mess o' it this time!"

There is no time for a Soviet response. Four points. No two teams can overtake Scotland. Scotland have qualified from the group stage! USSR can still equal the Scots total and perhaps overtake them on goal average but only if the Soviets beat Chile in their final game and Scotland lose to North Korea and what are the chances of that, after Scotland's first two performances? . . . . .

Chapter 20

Scotland are Goliath

Scotland v North Korea.

Ayresome Park.

19th July 1966.

T he final group matches in the World Cup are a creation of fiendish beauty. Almost every side can climb back into contention with a final game win. Teams that seem untouchable after opening game victories can find themselves slipping into third place. 85 minutes into their game with Scotland, USSR had looked assured of a qualifying place, now if Chile defeat them, they will leapfrog over the Soviets. If, at the same time, North Korea beat Scotland, the Koreans will tie with Chile on three points and goal average will come into play.

The only place to be, is safely above misadventure, with two wins out of two. The Scotland players sit at breakfast in their hotel relaxed, laughing and joking. Their final match against North Korea is a game they are expected to win and win well. Perhaps there is a kink in the Scottish psyche. The over-confident underdog, born from two phases of Scottish history, centuries as the underdog, fighting to resist English domination, followed by two hundred years of fortune-making through slavery and conquest as fully paid-up participants in the British Empire. We can never quite forget our two centuries as leaders of the world, nor that we gave the world so many of the engineering marvels of the Industrial Revolution and that our tough, skilled workmen spread football round the globe as we taught other nations how to build railways and ships.We can be slow to understand how quickly a pupil can outstrip a teacher.

Scotland are not always at their best in matches they expect to win.

Another aspect of the tie with North Korea is expressed in The Scotsman newspaper by Arthur Donaldson, chairman of the Scottish National Party. "Tonight, sees the unique occasion of two countries, unrecognized as nations by the British Government in Westminster, playing for a place in the Quarter Finals of the World Cup"

Jock Stein is determined that complacency does not blight the Scottish performance. The whole squad watched North Korea's opening game with USSR, the management team attended the 1-1 draw with Chile. The day before Scotland's game with North Korea, Stein's network of contacts pulls out another ace. He has his squad gather in the hotel function room. With him is a man in his mid-twenties, who looks like all the other players in the room, apart from his maroon and cream bowling shirt and suntan.

"Gentlemen, let me introduce to you, Archie Blue" Stein says, as Archie beams a friendly "G'day!" to the gathering. "Archie is a product of the Lanarkshire Juniors just as I am, except he had the misfortune to play for Larkhall Royal Albert and no' the mighty Blantyre Vics!". The group laughs at Stein's competitive humour. "Archie was also on Hearts' books and he's disappointed that his former clubmate Dave MacKay is away having his injury attended to." "Not sure that Dave would remember me," Archie interjects, "he was a big star. I didn't get a single first team game."

Stein continues, "After a career in Scotland and England, Archie headed down-under and won a place in the Australian National team." "Scored a hattrick against China." Archie adds with another smile. "Yes, indeed. Archie has been good enough to interrupt his holiday back home to come to speak with us, because who do you think knocked Australia out of this World Cup?"

"North Korea?" calls out Billy McNeil. "Yes, Billy, North Korea. So, Archie knows the Scottish game and the North Korean and he's agreed to give us a few pointers before tomorrow's match."

"Thank you, Mr. Stein. First of all, I'd just like tae say how thrilled I am to be here. It's an honour to help my country, if I can. North Korea? Most important thing I can tell you is: don't underestimate them. We did. We knew nothing about them and when we saw them, all about five feet six, we thought "We'll stuff this lot." It all went wrong for us and they beat us 6-1 and even when we knew better what to expect and gave a better account of ourselves, they still beat us 3-1, in the second leg. To be fair to my teammates can I explain a bit about where we played them?" Archie asks and Jock tells him, "Of course, go ahead."

"We were supposed to be a Rest of the World qualifying section, after 15 places in the Finals went to Europe and South America but the black African teams staged a boycott, angry that Africa didn't have a place in its own right and because South Africa were still in the competition. We were then put in a group with South Africa and North and South Korea but South Korea pulled out, in protest at North Korea being invited. Then South Africa were expelled, because of apartheid and that left only us and North Korea. Bit of a joke I know, especially after all the tough games you had to play to qualify. We just had to beat North Korea and Australia would be in the World Cup Finals." Archie rummages in a bag on the table in front of him and pulls out a tie, emblazoned with "Australia World Cup 1966". "We were so confident of winning, we even got these made before the match!" The Scottish players laugh as Archie holds up the tie. Archie continues. "Perhaps if we'd played them in Sydney we might have stood a chance but the Aussie Government has a policy against visitors from South East Asia. Not surprising since our boys are fighting and dying Vietnam. To cap it all, the Koreans didn't have a stadium that was good enough either. So, it was agreed that both games would take place in Cambodia. What a place! It was like going tae another planet and we were all feeling our bellies a bit off from the strange food. Anyway, whatever it was, we didnae stuff them, they stuffed us."

"Tell me, Archie" Stein asks, "how did they play? Were there any stand-out players? How did they deal with crosses and high balls, you being bigger than them?"

"Stand out players? That's no' so easy. They all look the same, for a start but also because they were all brilliant, every one of them. Fast, skillful, brave, couldn't be bullied off the ball. They attacked us every time they could. We found out after the game that they are an Army side, playing and working together for years. Maybe we did win a few in the air but they were after the layoffs like terriers. I guess they were a bit like that Scottish side of wee fellows, the Wembley Wizards, that beat England 5-1. Pak Do Ik, I remember, a fast skillful winger, like wee Willie here or Jimmy. Pak Seung Zin a goalscoring inside forward, onto the ball in a flash, like Denis. These are the names I remember best. Don't think you are going to win just because you're bigger than them. That's my advice. Imagine you're playing the Wembley Wizards!"

Stein thanks Archie and invites him to join the squad in the hotel bar in an hour when the briefing is finished. Archie is delighted.

While the squad relaxes in the bar, Stein meets the world's Press. He gives them the same answers he gave his players earlier that day, "There will be no complacency. There is a lot to play for. North Korea can still finish second if they beat us and other results go their way. Similarly, we are playing to stay in top spot. If we lose and the Soviets beat Chile, we could finish second."

"Mr Stein," asks Jim Rodger, "Scotland are Goliath in this match and North Korea are David, have you picked a tall side to physically intimidate the Koreans?"

"No, Jim," Stein replies, "if I was doing that, I would have picked Ron Yeats! No, we believe the Koreans will play with passion and skill and I've picked a team to match them in that. It's also our third game in 6 days, with a quarter final 4 days after, so I will make a few changes without weakening the team."

The next day, Scotland and North Korea are involved in one of the most amazing matches in World Cup history.

. . . .

The Ayresome Park fans have taken the North Koreans to their hearts. They have been impressed by their wholehearted, fast attacking play. The Koreans play in red, just as Middlesborough do and the local supporters have no time for Sunderland big-shot Baxter. All of this is of little significance as the locals in the stadium are outnumbered three to one by the Scottish support. It is as if Scotland are co-hosts. Every game is a home game to the Scots in this World Cup.

As announced in the Press conference, manager Jock Stein puts out a changed side: Lawrence, Gemmell, McCreadie, Greig, McNeil, Baxter, Henderson, W. Hamilton, Gilzean, Law and W. Johnston. On paper a fast, skillful attacking side chosen to take the game to the North Koreans.

Twenty-five minutes into the match and Jock Stein is crimson with rage. His team have heeded his instruction to play fast attacking football but he is sure he never told them to forget how to defend.

One minute into the game, Baxter's pass to set Johnston away is cut out by Kim Zoong-Sun, who plays the ball forward to Pak Do Ik. McCreadie lunges in but the little Korean steps inside him and rolls the ball to Pak Seung-Zin who languidly loops a left foot shot into Lawrence's top right hand corner. The Koreans' bouncing dance of delight is infectiously pleasing to all watching, apart from the fans and players of Scotland.

Scotland are stung and launch attack after attack in reply. Korean skipper, Shin Yung-Kyoo makes a lunging tackle to prevent Law from latching onto a Henderson cross. From the resultant corner a McNeil header is cleared off the line. Minutes later, Hamilton's twenty yard drive draws a fine diving save from Ri Chan Myung. The match swings from end to end, Lawrence makes a good save from Han Bong-Zin, then, a minute later, Henderson cuts inside and fires in a fierce shot that Myung in the Korean goal, tips over at full length. A Gilzean header results in another fine save and with twenty minutes played, Willie Johnston slices a drive over the bar.

In the opening twenty minutes, Scotland have had more chances than in their entire victory over USSR but in playing so openly they are exposing themselves to counter-attack. In twenty-two minutes Pak Do Ik floats over a ball that evades Gemmell. Yang Zeung-Kook on the Korean left wing dinks the ball back over Gemmell and Lawrence to the back post where Li Dong-Woon stabs home.

Scotland go back up the park in search of a goal back. Hamilton is tripped outside the box. Greig tries a twenty yard direct shot that flies narrowly past the post. The Scottish pressure must surely result in a goal, instead, in the twenty-fifth minute Yang Zeung-Kook dances past Gemmell and McNeil to fire home a third goal for North Korea. Stein watches on in furious disbelief. The world's press and commentators report with glee the stunning achievement of the unknown underdogs.

There are no substitutes and Scotland have sent out a team with no hard tackling midfielders, their only way out of an unbelievable 3 goal deficit is to continue to attack in an effort to outscore their opponents. Two minutes after the third Korean goal, Baxter plays in Gilzean. There is a moment's indecision as two Korean defenders are uncertain which one should go for the ball. It is the opening the Tottenham striker needs as he sweeps the ball into the net.

It is 3-1 at half-time. Jock Stein realizes that his team selection is partly to blame. Gemmell looks less comfortable at right back and the midfield would have offered the defence more cover if Bremner, Murdoch or even the unavailable MacKay had played. He switches McCreadie and Gemmell but he cannot ask Baxter or Hamilton to play the midfield ball-winner, instead he asks them to keep the ball from the Koreans as much as possible. Frustrate them, dominate them and keep playing for openings and the goals will surely come.

Scotland do dominate the second half. The Koreans shift from pure attacking football to a more desperate, at times illegal, defence of their lead. Free kicks and two overruled penalty claims follow, until the 56th minute when Hamilton slots a through ball to Gilzean, who in a mirror image of his first goal, reduces the deficit to one.

Gemmell rampages forward in his more natural position of left back, Myung, the excellent Korean keeper, tips a long range Gemmell drive over the bar. Scotland have the players to keep taking the game to their opponents and the pressure pays off in the 80th minute, when a Henderson cross to the far post is met by Denis Law whose header draws the teams level.

In the closing ten minutes the North Koreans try to create a final opportunity. They know that only a win offers them a chance of qualifying but Scotland have the measure of them by now and finish the game looking the more likely to score. The referee blows the final whistle, bringing to a close an astounding first twenty five minutes, followed by a skilled and determined recovery by the Scots.

"Well played, lads," Stein tells his team at the end, "just don't bloody well dare gi'e another team a three goal lead in this competition!"

• •

Chapter 21

The Soccer star who doesn't have to leave home to play in the World Cup.

Quarter Finals.

Scotland v Hungary

23rd July 1966.

Roker Park, Sunderland.

The final group games produce the teams that will meet in the Quarter Finals and contest the knockout stage of the competition.

Playing all their games at Wembley, England beat France 2-0 to top Group One. Uruguay play out their second 0-0 draw in three games to secure runner-up in the group.

West Germany come back from 1-0 down against Spain, to win 2-1 with an 84th minute Uwe Seeler goal. Argentina defeat Switzerland 2-0, to tie on 5 points with the Germans. West Germany's 5-0 mauling of the Swiss in game one sees them top the group on goal average.

With the winners of Group One playing the runners up of Group Two, England will face Argentina and West Germany will play Uruguay.

In Group Three Portugal defeat Brazil 3-1 with Eusebio outgunning a limping Pele, while Hungary beat Bulgaria to secure second place in the group. In Group Four USSR beat Chile 2-1 to qualify a point behind Scotland.

As winners of Group 3 Portugal will face USSR in the Quarter Final.

Scotland return to their home from home, Roker Park, to play Hungary in their Quarter Final tie.

Just as at the draw for the Finals in January, with no disrespect to any team, Jock Stein cannot suppress the knowledge that he'd rather face Hungary than any other team left in the competition.

Jim Baxter's feeling that it is all meant to be is growing. Back to Roker Park for the Quarter Final. The squad will stay on a further few days in their Gateshead base. A squad of immensely talented players who have now been together for three weeks and are beginning to react and play like a club side. More than that, with the games coming so thick and fast, it is the fittest Jim has been for a year, the least he's had to drink in a month since he left Raith Rovers.

In the squad and in the nation the feeling is growing. Two games from the World Cup Final. Two home games. Who's going to stop them?

Jock Stein likes to create any psychological advantage he can. He wants the Hungarians to fear how relaxed and at home the Scots are. On 20th July he has the Press attend a light-hearted training match, capturing pictures of Denis Law, blonde head tilted back, laughing, next to the diminutive mischievous wingers, Henderson and Johnstone. The next day, Stein allows the players a second shopping trip or meet up with their wives. Jim Baxter is allowed to visit his Sunderland home on condition that he does a photo shoot for the Press and on condition that he is back to the hotel for 9pm. Neil Mochan is detailed to stay nearby to make sure the return is achieved.

The picture that the Daily Record syndicates to the world is Jim Baxter on his sofa at home, legs outstretched, smiling, hand held out to accept a cup of tea from Jean, his wife. "The Soccer Star who doesn't have to leave home to play in the World Cup" the headline says. "This World Cup is turning out better than I could ever have hoped," Jim tells the reporter, "who widnae want tae play all your games at home?"

Stein is pleased with the picture and pleased when Jim turns up, only mildly tipsy, in Neil Mochan's car at 8.55pm.

. . . .

"Hungary cannot be underestimated." Stein tells his players. "In Ferenc Bene and Florian Albert they have two of the best forwards in the tournament. They beat Brazil 3-1. We will have to be at our best to win."

Stein also knows to win he needs to find his best formation. Simpson in goal, Greig to play the attacking right back role he performed so well against Italy, Gemmell to be himself as attacking left back. Ronnie McKinnon, perhaps the best natural defender in the squad, to partner Billy McNeil. Billy Bremner to provide bite and skill in midfield, alongside Bobby Murdoch and Jim Baxter. A winger will have to be sacrificed but with such strong overlapping full backs, Baxter and Murdoch will still have players to hit with their passes. Gilzean and Law worked well against North Korea. Is Jinky still too much of a one-man-band for what will have to be a strong team performance? Wee Willie Henderson it is then.

Roker Park is once again a sea of Scotland fans. Jim Baxter spreads a nerveless confidence that infuses the quiet determination of his colleagues. Jock Stein has talked through the Hungarian danger men and every Scottish player knows his task. From first minute to last it becomes apparent that the Hungarians of '66 reached their peak against Brazil, where keeper Gelei made many splendid saves, Ferenc Bene weaved his way to an excellent goal, Albert thrust repeatedly through the Brazilian defence and Farkas finished a flowing move with a volley. Against Scotland they never reach these heights. Gemmell controls Bene. McKinnon and McNeil dominate Albert. Bremner and Murdoch tackle effectively in front of the defence and Baxter links defence and attack with precision passing, short and long. Five minutes into the game, Willie Henderson, starting on the left to confuse the Hungarians, cuts inside Hungarian right back Beno Kaposzta to fire in a low hard shot. Gelie saves but in doing so spills the ball, an invitation Denis Law cannot resist as he slides in to knock ball and goalkeeper into the net. Three minutes into the second half, Baxter glides down the left flank, chips into the box where centre half Kalman Maszoly heads the ball over his keeper's arms straight into the path of Gilzean who heads into the empty net. Bene does evade Gemmell to shoot home on the hour but Scotland's tactical set-up and skilled play denies the Magyars many openings. The only blemish on a professional performance is a Sandor Matrai foul on Henderson in the dying minutes that sees the winger limp off with an ankle injury.

Although he tries to disguise it, Jock Stein purrs with delight at the game's end, not only are they through to the World Cup semi-final, he has found the formation that suits this squad of players best.

• •

Chapter 22

For John White

Scotland v West Germany.

World Cup semi-final.

25th July 1966.

Goodison Park.

"**I** need tae keep the heid" Jock Stein tells Sean Fallon and Neil Mochan in the hotel bar after the victory over Hungary.

"Keep the players' excitement in check, you mean?" Sean asks. "To stop them getting carried away?"

"No." Jock replies, "Myself. My own excitement. I can feel my heart racing. To get so close."

"No-one could fault ye, Jock" Mochan interjects, "We've got so far.."

"I know, Neilly, I know." Stein replies, "If someone had offered me the semi-final when we started the qualification campaign, the first game against Finland, I would have bitten their hand off but not now we're here. Not now we've got so close. Only two games away. Can you believe it?"

Fallon feels a sense of unease amid the jubilation, "You're no thinking of taking this job full time are you, Jock?!"

Stein looks through his assistant with a disbelieving stare, "You know me better than that, Sean! I gave Mr. Kelly my word.

Winning the league at Celtic is only the start, I have so much work to do. I feel a big season coming on. Ach, this World Cup is a dream. Five games in ten days. A full time international boss is no' for me. Five games a year? Meeting other managers' players for a day or two beforehand? Get awa' wi' you!" Fallon nods acceptance of his boss's angry words, Stein continues," But these days, this chance, we may never have it again. The-World-Cup-Semi-Final. I need tae keep the heid."

Sean and Neil nod that they understand. Understand the enormity, the achievement, the opportunity.

Neil Mochan has always been mischievous. "And ye ken what makes it worse?" he asks, waiting for Jock and Sean to tell him to go on, "We have better players than any other team left in this cup!"

• •

23rd July 1966. World Cup Quarter Finals. In venues spread across England, the South Americans and the Communists are sent home. Scotland beat Hungary. Portugal beat USSR 2-1. England play an angry match with Argentina. Rattin, the Argentinian captain, is sent off for refusing to stop intimidating the referee. His team try to walk off in protest before they are told, if they do so, they forfeit the match. Hurst scores a late winner for England. Alf Ramsey loses his usual cool and calls the Argentinians "Animals" and wrestles an England shirt out of George Cohen's hands, as he tries to exchange it with an Argentinian opponent. Meanwhile, at Hillsborough, Sheffield, West Germany beat Uruguay 4-0. The Uruguayans who looked so hard to break down in the group games. The match tells a not straightforward story. Uruguay hit the bar, then have shot handled on the line by Schnellinger, with the penalty denied. Only after that they lose their control, have two players sent off. Players who have to be ushered from the field, still complaining, by the police. Against nine men, Germany rack up their score.

The Semi-Final draw is pre-arranged. 25th July. England versus

Portugal at Goodison Park, Liverpool. Scotland versus West Germany at Wembley.

24th July the politics begins.
. . . .

"Jock, Jock, they've switched the venues!" Neil Mochan runs in with a small transistor radio in hand. "It's on the news! England will play Portugal at Wembley and we're to play at Goodison Park. They say it's to accommodate the extra numbers of England fans."

"Ach, getaway!" Jock retorts, "Does anyone seriously think that Scotland canna fill Wembley?!"

"Maybe that's exactly what they don't want" comments Sean Fallon, centuries of Irish history in his mind.

The phone rings. Jock answers. Willie Allan from the SFA confirming the news. Stein replaces the receiver. "Just as well we've not relocated south yet" he says. "Goodison it is. One venue's as good as another."
. . . .

Arthur Donaldson from the SNP cannot help but notice the growing number of slights. He writes in "The Scotsman" newspaper, "First it was "World Cup Willie" the mascot with the Union Flag emblazoned on his chest. "It is because we have two countries from the United Kingdom in the competition" the organizers hastily dissembled. Then they saw that all England fans wave not the St George's Cross but, once again, the Union Flag. The flag of the four so-called equal partners in the United Kingdom. Scotland, Wales, Northern Ireland and England. The English cannot believe, indeed do not understand, that they are not Britain. Now, the final insult. Due to the excellent play from both Home Nations, both England and Scotland are in the semi-finals. Scotland drawn at Wembley. "No, they are not Britain, I mean, England" the organizers cry. "We cannot have them here, spoiling our tournament, our celebration of nationhood." That is, perhaps, the greatest irony. The English have a great sense of their own identity. A great conceit of their nationhood. Yet England cannot truly be accounted a nation unless they simultaneously agree to let Scotland go free!"

• •

West Germany versus Scotland. Scotland have never lost to West Germany. Won two, drawn one. Never lost to united Germany before the war, either. Drew in Berlin, 1929, beat them in Glasgow during Hitler's Reich, 1937.

The first stadium where there will be ten thousand opposition fans. Sure, there will be 40,000 Scottish fans but the Germans will be noisy with their trademark horns. Got to hope the 8,000 scousers will be on Scotland's side.

Strong, skillful, arrogant, manipulative, never-say-die opponents: Tilkowski, Lutz, Schnellinger, Beckenbauer, Schulz, Weber, Held, Overath, Seeler, Haller and Emmerich. Beat Switzerland 5-0, Uruguay 4-0. Not a team to be messed with.

Stein knows his best side, how he wants to play the Germans. One hour from kick-off, inside the away changing room in Goodison Park, he plays his final card.

Stein has asked the boys to all be changed early. Into the room comes Dave MacKay on crutches. Back with the squad but no chance of playing before tournament's end. He brings with him a slim, pretty 25-year-old woman, holding the hand of a four year old girl. Crowding in behind them is Bill Brown, reserve goalkeeper, holding the hand of a two-year-old boy.

Stein stands to command attention, "Lads, lads! Please welcome back Dave MacKay and with him, the widow and children of his former clubmate, John White. Sandra White and her children, Mandy and Rob. Sandra and the children have been good enough to interrupt their annual trip up north to stay with Granny White in Musselburgh, isn't that right, Sandra?"

The team are dumbstruck. The woman and children in front of them are all so young. Sandra tries to help them feel more comfortable. "We've come to wish you all the best," she says in her lilting Welsh voice. Then her voice breaks, "John would have wanted you so very much to win."

Jock Stein speaks, "John White, so many of you played alongside. He made his first international appearance in 1959 in a 3-2 victory over West Germany. He made his last international appearance in May 1964 in a 2-2 away draw with West Germany. Gillie, you scored two goals against the Germans that night." Young Mandy clings to her mother's legs but Bill Brown has let go the hand of toddler Rob, who is charmingly going round and shaking every player's hand. Jim Baxter feels a tear run down his cheek. Jock Stein continues. "No-one could have foreseen that game in Germany would be John's last Scotland match. No-one could have foreseen the tragedy. John would have played with you in the qualification games. Have no doubt, John would have been in the squad alongside you now. In the team, I don't doubt. He was one of us. One of you. And he had this chance taken from him. The chance you all have now. Sandra, Mandy, Rob, thank you so very much for coming. It means so much as you can see. Sandra, any last words?"

Sandra too wipes a tear from her eye. She has worked so hard to move on with her life, for her own sake and the children's but the sight of the seated rectangle of young footballers, in the same dark blue Scotland shirts that John was so proud to wear, that sight is too much for her. Sandra hasn't seen John since he inexplicably sat under a tree, yet in that moment she thinks she catches a glimpse of him, out the corner of her eye, in his Scotland kit, smiling, at her, the children and all the players around him. Sandra raises the fingers of her left hand to her mouth as she intakes a breath. The image disappears.

"John would have so loved to be here," Sandra tells the Scotland team. "So much have wanted to be playing alongside you in this match." Sandra feels the tears and the loss of control. "Win this game for John White" she sobs, "win this game for my John."

Dave MacKay and Bill Brown feel an overwhelming sense of responsibility and concern for the family of their fallen teammate, "We'll see you to your seats, Sandra." MacKay says, then he turns back to his international colleagues. "So many of us came so close against the Czechs in 1961, now you've got the chance to go so much further. Win this game, lads. Win it for John White."

Jock Stein started off believing he had orchestrated a morale boosting ploy but as he feels the emotion in the room and senses the presence of the Ghost of White Hart Lane, he says, "You heard them, lads. Win it for John White!"

• •

Willie Henderson's ankle knock against Hungary rules him out of the match. "It's time," Jock tells his assistants, "to unleash Jimmy Johnstone on this tournament." "Jimmy will have the beating of Schnellinger." Stein tells his players. "For all his reputation, he won't have played against a Jimmy Johnstone before. Give the ball to Jinky."

This World Cup has been an amazing tournament, testing the physical and psychological endurance of all the young athletes involved. Games every two or three days, each one bigger than the last, each successive game the most important match any of them has ever played. In such a pressure cooker a team needs a strong guiding manager, dedicated players at the peak of their careers and nerves of steel. "We can win this." Jim Baxter tells his teammates as they rise to enter the tunnel.

The World Cup Semi-Final against West Germany. A team needs to play its natural game. A team needs to not be overawed. Could Simpson, Greig, Gemmell, Murdoch, McNeil, McKinnon, Johnstone, Bremner, Gilzean, Law and Baxter ever be overawed?

Accompanied by the roars of the Scots and the klaxons of the Germans, this match between two heavyweights begins at a frantic pace. Three minutes into the game, Murdoch releases an overlapping Greig, who unleashes a twenty-yard shot. Tilkowski only parries the ball to the feet of the inrushing Johnstone who thumps home.

The Germans, led by their rising young star, Franz Beckenbauer, like to present a cool, invulnerable front but the Scottish attack is troubling them. The movement of Gilzean and Law, the passing of Murdoch, Bremner and Baxter, the thrusting runs of Greig and Gemmell and the unpredictable chaos of Jimmy Johnstone tying left back Schnellinger's legs in knots. Scotland dominate but Germany with Held and Emmerich on the wings, Beckenbauer, Haller and Overath in midfield are capable of their own attacks. On 38 minutes an Emmerich corner is only half cleared allowing Beckenbauer to stab the ball into the net.

In the second half both teams press for the winner. Tommy Gemmell smashes the crossbar with a shot. Tilkowski dives at the feet of first Law then Gilzean as they come within inches of collecting penetrating passes from Baxter. One hour played Weber launches a high ball forward. Seeler and McNeil prepare to jump for the ball, except Billy doesn't jump as he is laid low by Seeler's slamming elbow. The Italian referee sees nothing wrong as Helmut Haller latches onto Seeler's uncontested head flick. 2-1 to West Germany.

Four minutes later Seeler trips McKinnon as he looks to launch an attack. Everyone takes responsibility in this Scotland team. Ronnie picks himself up, sees Alan Gilzean ready to attack the ball, McKinnon floats in a quick free-kick, Gilzean heads home.

The final twenty minutes becomes ever more physical. Nine minutes from time Emmerich runs onto a long Tilkowski kick but Ronnie Simpson makes a great save from his rasping drive.

Two minutes from time, Baxter slips the ball to Tommy Gemmell, who steps inside the challenge of Lutz. On toward the German goal Gemmell weaves. Haller makes no attempt to play the ball as he slides into Gemmell's legs from behind. Gemmell stumbles but regains his balance, in a stride, before unleashing a twenty yard shot that flashes past Tilkowski's despairing dive. Gemmell is mobbed by his teammates yet still has time, as he returns to his own half, to tell Haller, "Serves you right, ya cheating bastard!"

There is no time for the Germans to score their trademark last minute goal. A thrilling, draining, bruising encounter. Scotland are through to the World Cup Final.

• •

Chapter 23

Who gave Football to the World?

Scotland v England.

World Cup Final.

30th July 1966.

Wembley Stadium, London.

Between 1957 and 1962 Alf Ramsey takes unfashionable Ipswich Town from the Third Division to being Champions of England. In May 1963 he becomes England manager. Ramsey is the sort of managerial appointment that Scotland should have made at that time; a full time manager, given full control of team selection without interference from F.A selectors. In 1960 England are chosen to host the World Cup, so Ramsey's appointment is made with the 1966 home tournament in mind. In his first Press conference Ramsey confidently predicts that England will win the World Cup in 3 years time. A prediction he repeats as the tournament nears.

Ramsey has grown up in poverty in Dagenham, a rural village at the time. Wartime service, where he rises to be a quartermaster sergeant in Britain and Palestine teaches him discipline and how to conduct himself socially, a skill that does not come easily to him. Ramsey's best playing years are with Tottenham and England. He carries a scar above his lip from a childhood boxing match and a scar on the inside from being in the England team that loses 1-0 to the United States in the 1950 World Cup. Ramsey is literally a self-made man, who claims to be two years younger than he is for the majority of his career and who takes elocution lessons to refine his Dagenham accent. Ramsey will ensure that discipline and meticulous planning will give his team the best chance of success. He is not an easy man to intimidate. During England's World Cup group match with France, Nobby Stiles is booked for a high challenge that injures France's Jacky Simon. FIFA put pressure on the English FA, who ask Ramsey if he will omit Stiles from the rest of the tournament. "Yes, you could drop Nobby Stiles but if you did, you would be looking for a new manager in the middle of an international tournament, of which we are the prestigious hosts, which might be a little inconvenient." Ramsey replies.

On 26th July 1966 England defeat Portugal 2-1 to reach the World Cup Final. Ramsey's England enter the Final on an excellent run of form. Unbeaten in 16 games, with thirteen wins and three draws since October 1965, England have conceded only 7 goals in these games, three of them against Scotland in April. Ramsey has found his formation, 4-4-2 or 4-3-3, "wingless wonders", first adopted in a 2-0 defeat of Spain in Madrid in December 1965. Ramsey has also single-mindedly found his team, with England's leading scorer, Jimmy Greaves, being the most controversial omission.

In the four days between the semi-final and final, Ramsey remains confident, although he suppresses the small voice inside his head that says, "Scotland. Scotland. Why did it have to be Scotland?"

Jock Stein also knows his formation and his team. He sees no reason to change the eleven that did so well in the semi-final against West Germany. His task is to manage the disappointment of the eleven left out, or more particularly the three or four who may have thought they had a chance of playing. McCreadie, St John and Lennox who all played in earlier matches. Stein tells the whole 22 they have played an important part in making Scotland's run to the Final such a success. They are all patriotic Scotsmen but those left out will be among the few of their countrymen, who will watch the final with a tinge of regret.

27th July and Scotland relocate to the Brent Bridge Hotel in Hendon, a short bus journey from Wembley. Remarkably they are only a few miles from their opponents, the England team in Hendon Hall. The logistics create a unique event when by sheer coincidence a group of players from both teams end up at the same cinema in Golders Green on the evening of the 28th, watching "Those Magnificent Men in their Flying Machines". A single lucky Press photographer gets a snap of the mingled group, Bremner, Law and Baxter next to Moore, Peters and Hurst, as they leave the cinema. "Those Magnificent Men and the Hopes of their Nations" is the caption used. In contrast to some of the more bullish reporting in the English Press, the accompanying article, stresses that whatever the result on Saturday the final will be a triumph for Britain.

Baxter comes away from the encounter telling the rest of the Scotland squad, "See they English boys, we've got them running scared!"

Remarkably, considering Scotland have only lost one of the last five encounters between the teams, the English Press is generally hostile and dismissive of the Scots. Desmond Hackett of the Daily Express writes, "England will firmly relegate Scotland back to their minor role in international football. I don't know why the Scots are even bothering to turn up. If Scotland win, I will eat my hat." Brian James in the Daily Mirror writes, "The Scots have no chance, they have not learned as much about football as England."

Jock Stein pins both articles to the training room wall. It is all the motivation the Scotland team need.

The Daily Telegraph runs an article entitled "Inexperienced Scots" with pictures of Simpson, Gemmell, Murdoch, McKinnon and Johnstone, the players in the expected team with less than ten caps. "Auld Faither" Ronnie Simpson raises a laugh from the squad when he exclaims, "Inexperienced! I was at Wembley in 1948 with the British Olympic team!" Some in the room are not sure if Simpson is joking, "and I won the FA Cup there, twice, with Newcastle in '52 and '55. Inexperienced my arse."

There is also a florid article in The Times declaring it is England's destiny to win in the Final as just reward for giving Football to the World. "Aye," growls Stein to the players, "how many of those pioneers were Scots? I can tell ye that in the fifteen matches between Scotland and England after the first game in 1873, Scotland won 10, drew 3 and lost only two. 48 goals to 27. Who's teaching who? But forget all that ancient history, it's what you do tomorrow that counts."

"What score would you like, boss?" Pipes up Baxter. "I was thinking 3-2 to Scotland has a nice ring tae it!"

Stein has a momentary memory of the words attributed to William Wallace, "I've brocht ye tae the ring, now dance as best ye can." Except that was before a defeat. Seventeen hours before kick-off and he has never seen a group of players so confident and relaxed.

• •

Stein feels his shoulders relax. The team has shaken hands with the Queen with great dignity and no nonsense. The Stadium appears to be evenly split between the two sets of supporters, despite the smaller Scottish allocation. The occasion is majestic. Billy McNeil and Bobby Moore have led out their teams into the cauldron, like the elegant young gladiators they are. Stein wipes a bead of sweat off his forehead. There is nothing more he can do. The game is on.

35 million viewers in Britain, 400 million worldwide, listen to Kenneth Wolstenholme read out the teams; Banks, Cohen, Wilson, Stiles, Charlton.J, Moore, Ball, Hunt, Charlton.R, Hurst and Peters. Against: Simpson, Greig, Gemmell, Murdoch, McNeil, McKinnon, Johnstone, Bremner, Gilzean, Law and Baxter. A bright summer's day overhead, no clash of colours, England in white, Scotland in blue. The only clash, perhaps, in temperament and footballing

philosophy.

England do not have the first half they hope for because Scotland don't let them. Greig, Gemmell, Bremner, McNeil and Murdoch all tackle incisively. Ronnie McKinnon completely dominates Geoff Hurst. From this strong defensive platform, Scotland launch wave after wave of fast skillful attacks, with Jim Baxter always at the heart of the build up. England simply don't have a similar player who can take the ball from his own penalty area and pass and move it forward toward the opposition's danger area. The other factor that hampers England is a clash in 13 minutes between Jack Charlton and Alan Gilzean. Charlton's boot connects with Gilzean's knee with such force that the stud punctures the inner-sole and breaks Jack's toe. After treatment Gilzean continues but Charlton is off the field for eleven minutes, his foot being bound up by Harold Shepherdson and Les Cocker. When Jack returns he plays up front with Stiles moving back alongside Bobby Moore. Despite Charlton's obvious limp he goes on to have more scoring chances than any other player on the park.

For all that Scotland appear the more energetic and inventive side, both teams fashion chances. On 17 Minutes Ronnie Simpson saves well from Hurst, two minutes later Bobby Charlton finally manages a trademark weaving surge from midfield but his shot goes over. A minute after that, down the other end, Bremner pushes a free-kick to Greig who drives narrowly wide. Then the best chance, both keepers are preferring short throw outs to big kicks, Banks rolls the ball to Wilson who is caught in possession close to his bye-line by Johnstone, the cross flashes across goal but Law, at full stretch can only shoot into the side net.

On 28 minutes Scotland achieve the breakthrough. Bremner charges down a Peters' pass, in the ensuing race for the loose ball, Peters obstructs the Leeds player. Bremner plays a quick free-kick to Baxter who moves the ball across to Johnstone. Johnstone shoots, Banks saves but can only parry the ball into the path of Law who scores. With only half an hour on the clock the 50,000 Scottish fans begin to chant "Easy, Easy"

Except it isn't easy. England do not want to lose on such a big occasion. Jack Charlton heads over from a Moore cross, minutes later Charlton connects with a Stiles cross forcing Simpson to save. On 39 minutes Hunt is released by a one-two with Hurst, Simpson saves his near post shot. Two minutes later Baxter feeds Bremner who sets Denis Law free in the box but Banks and Stiles combine to cut him out. ITV viewers hear Billy Wright tell commentator Hugh Johns, "England are working hard to overcome Charlton's injury but Scotland are in full song"

Referee Schulenberg blows for half-time. The Scots have played as well as anyone could have hoped in the first 45 minutes, yet it has still been an end to end game. Scotland have had six shots off target and three on, while England have had four chances on target and three off. Scotland have the vital first goal. Jock Stein tells his players to produce one similar 45 minutes of football and the World Cup will be theirs.

England start the second half stronger, stung by Alf Ramsey's warning that they risk losing everything they have all worked so hard for. Alan Ball weaves past three challenges, passes to Jack Charlton, whose shot is stopped by Ronnie Simpson on the line, with England players claiming it is over. "The linesman is in the best position," Billy Wright reminds viewers.

Two minutes later, Bobby Charlton again manages a rampage through the middle, releasing Hunt with his pass but once again Simpson saves. The game swings from chance to chance. Gemmell shoots over, Jack Charlton heads over, on the hour mark Stiles clatters into Gemmell in the box but the referee sees shoulder to shoulder. Peters heads wide from a Cohen cross and with 70 minutes played Jack Charlton again gets in a header which beats Simpson, with John Greig heading off the line. Greig clenches his fist in a gesture of celebration and determination not to let slip this opportunity of a lifetime.

The next goal will be crucial. Hurst finally evades McKinnon to create space for a shot, which Simpson dives to save. The play moves to the other end. Law and Stiles tussle for the ball, Schulenberg blows for a foul against Stiles. Both Manchester United men shrug their shoulders not knowing what was wrong. Baxter passes to Gemmell, whose shot is headed out by Moore. The clearance falls kindly for Gemmell who finds Johnstone on the edge of the box, Jinky passes inside to Gilzean, who sweeps the ball across Banks to enter the net off the far post.

Ten minutes to play and Scottish belief surges round the stadium. McNeil tackles Hurst, he passes the ball to Law, who backheels to Murdoch, who backheels to Baxter, who takes the ball for a wee keepy-uppy walk for three or four strides. The English can't get near him. Baxter lofts the ball over the English defence to Law, who controls on his chest but his cross is cut out.

England are a hurt and goaded bull. Ronnie Simpson cuts out every high or low ball they fire in, until the 85th minute when Hunt and Ball play a one-two, with Ball crossing for Jack Charlton to score. 2-1 and everything still to play for. A minute later McKinnon makes yet another strong but fair challenge on Hurst. Scotland break forward, Gemmell puts through Law, whose first-time chip almost clears Banks, who claws the ball away.

The England fans, who have been out-sung all day, burst into "England, England!" in a desperate attempt to inspire their team to an equalizer. With three minutes remaining, Billy Bremner breaks up an England attack. Bremner surges into space, passing to Gilzean, who passes to an onrushing Murdoch. Murdoch evades the last England defenders through a neat one-two with Johnstone before slotting the ball away at Banks' far post. 3-1 and the chants turn to "Scotland, Scotland!" followed by the taunting "Easy, Easy!"

Still England do not give up, cannot give up, on this their home final, the culmination of their dream. One minute after Scotland's goal, Jack Charlton crosses to Hurst who steers his header beyond Simpson. 3-2. England try final despairing attacks in search of the third goal but the Scotland defence holds firm. Mister Schulenberg blows the final whistle.

Neil Mochan shakes Jock Stein's hand, "My God, Jock. What have we done?!"

The England players are in despair. Jack Charlton kneels by the centre circle, his head in his hands, his brother Bobby is crying, he was meant to win today for the players lost at Munich 1958. Alf Ramsey has the decency to shake Stein's hand "Congratulations. Well done." He says before he goes onto the pitch to console his players and raise Jack Charlton from his knees.

A few jubilant Scotland fans spill onto the pitch but there is no mass invasion, the Queen is present and the cup still to be presented. The commentators, Wolstenholme and Johns, change for supporting England to saying what a great day this has been for Britain, a marvelous match marred only by the injury to Jack Charlton, which reduced England to ten men.

The Scottish players hug each other in delight. Two fans embrace Jim Baxter so fiercely he needs a policeman's help to break free. John Greig finds his former Rangers teammate, "We did it, Jim" and before Baxter can reply, Denis Law comes bouncing into the group, "We did it! We fucking beat them!" Law yells in ecstasy. Jock Stein is now on the pitch, shaking hands and embracing all his players. Stein and Baxter stop for a split second to regard each other. "I telt ye we could win it!" Baxter says with a grin.

"You did, Jim, you did." Stein replies, "And you gave me the year I asked for, thank you." The two men embrace. Rarely has there been two such different men, united in common cause.

The England team has to endure the agony of ascending the steps and coming back down without the cup. The ever gallant Bobby Moore wipes his hands before shaking the Queen's hand to receive his runners-up medal. Denis Law has a consoling arm for Nobby Stiles on his return to the pitch and a handshake for Bobby Charlton. Ramsey ensures the England team stays to clap the Scots as they mount the Wembley staircase. All of the Scotland team has played an exceptional game and a wonderful tournament. Willie

Allan in the stand cannot contain his glee. What a victory and a "home" tournament for Scotland without the expense. As the players go up the steps they are congratulated by Bill Shankly and Matt Busby in the stand.

Billy McNeil approaches the Queen and the Jules Rimet trophy. McNeil has been a great captain but it could be any of the eleven, who have played as captains all. No-one could have argued if the trophy had been handed to Jim Baxter. McNeil shakes hands with Sir Stanley Rous, then with the Queen before he turns with the golden trophy and raises his arm to show the 50,000 delirious Scotland fans in the stadium, the Jules Rimet Trophy, the World Cup.

At the celebratory banquet, after the match, Jock Stein once again finds himself next to Jim Baxter. "What will you do now, Jock?" Baxter asks.

"I'll no' stay on as Scotland manager," Stein states, "I feel a big season coming on with Celtic. All the domestic trophies to play for and our first attempt at the European Cup. What about you, Jim?"

Baxter smiles, no malice intended, not even toward himself, "Well, you know me, Jock. I've gi'ed ye the year you asked for, now I'm awa tae get drunk!"

Chapter 24

1966

Author's Note

J ack Charlton kneeling near the centre circle, his head in his hands, his brother Bobby crying, Nobby Stiles, socks round ankles, teeth out, skipping with the cup, Bobby Moore looking golden in the sun, barely any dirt on his shirt, raised onto the shoulders of his teammates, arm raised high holding the Jules Rimet Trophy. Alf Ramsey, almost no pictures of him with the cup because he does not believe it is his place to detract attention from the players. Instead, he goes round each player individually, shaking them by the hand "Well played. You should be enormously proud. Thank you for all you have done."

I have no psychological need to take the '66 World Cup from England. If you are an England supporter offended by the premise of this book, remember you have the ultimate effective retort. The truth.

If there was a moral driver to this story, it might be entitled "The Trial of Walter Skocik." All the Scottish eyewitness accounts describe a deliberate assault. Not a professional foul in a meaningful phase of play, nor revenge for a previous foul but the pathetic rage of an inferior opponent humiliated and out-played. I believe, as set out in the novel, that his "tackle" on Jim Baxter had profound negative effects on Baxter, Rangers and Scotland. Yes, Baxter returned to playing within a remarkably quick three months but the break brought about the end of the first golden period of Baxter's career. He played the odd good game after that but was never the same dominating world star, week in week out, that he had been before the injury. He missed the European Cup ties with Inter Millan and the World Cup qualification games against Poland. It was Scotland's draw and defeat to Poland that cost them their chance to play in the World Cup. A World Cup on their doorstep. Had Baxter, at his unbroken best, played in these games the outcome just might have been that little bit different, as set out in this book. I know it's not truth but I do believe that what I have set out is plausible. Scotland do not operate within fine margins of international footballing success anymore. They are nowhere near being a top team but in the 1960s they were. Unleash them on the World Cup in the familiar surroundings of England, with a massive support behind their back, well, you've just read what could easily have happened.

To factor in the impact of a continuously fit and confident Jim Baxter, I tried to change as little as possible in writing this book. He still goes to Sunderland, as his rift with Rangers over wages was too deep. He doesn't get a big club better suited to his talents because his off-field reputation is too off-putting. Sunderland obtain only two points more as a result of having a better Baxter.

It moves them from 19th to 13th and makes Baxter joint top scorer, when he was, in reality, a creditable one goal behind Martin and Mulhall. It is with Scotland, in the big games that brought the best out of Jim, with players better attuned to his vision and passing, that an uninterrupted Baxter makes the biggest difference. It is still a small difference, one goal versus Poland away, two goals versus Poland at home. Every other result remains the same. It might have happened.

For the World Cup Finals, I used some real games as the basis of the Scotland matches. The Final is, of course, the '67 game. You can watch the whole 1967 match for free on You Tube. Baxter's performance, in the first half in particular, is immense. I am sure he is mentioned by the commentator more often than Peters, Ball and Bobby Charlton combined and this is Baxter in decline, playing his last noteworthy game.

The semi-final is a version of the 1969 Scotland West Germany match, with Tommy Gemmell finally getting more effective revenge than booting Helmut Haller up the backside (much as this remains one of my favourite footballing memories!). Of course, in this alternative universe, the 1969 game in Hamburg never happens because Scotland qualify for Mexico 1970 as holders.

I started primary school in 1966. I am indebted to my older brothers for creating my interest in the players in this book. Their annuals and football year books were always about the house. By the age of 8, I remember Jim Baxter as an overweight man with a Mexican moustache on his return to Rangers, not the slim Jim of 5 years before. My own need to search out Scottish football injustices and counter-factual "what might have been" was born amid the absolute torture that was Argentina '78. My brother and I travelled to Anfield to support Scotland in the qualifying victory over Wales. I truly saw no reason why a squad that could field players playing in European finals could not give a good account of themselves in the World Cup. At the time my despair focused on why Ally McLeod did not play Derek Johnstone against Iran, after DJ's two great headed goals in the warm up games. As I was by then a young adult and scoring lots of goals as a fast, strong striker in University football, my trauma over Argentina mutated into a prolonged fantasy about a much improved version of myself bursting onto the scene to make the difference needed to get Scotland out of a tournament group stage. Despite the ticker-tape, the hostile reception in Buenos Aires and the speed and skill of Mario Kempes, Scotland win in '78.

I have to say that this book, with only minor changes to results and its cast of authentic world-class players, has proven to be a much more plausible and satisfying counter-factual story.

Finally, the heart of this book became the relationship between Jock Stein and Jim Baxter. In reality, Stein did not do well as Scotland manager in 1965. He failed in the task he set himself. As manager and player, Stein and Baxter only had in common one competitive game, the victory over Italy. So this book explores how Stein and Baxter, might have responded to a more prolonged exposure to each other, with Jim, without the leg break, not dipping in form as swiftly as he did. Perhaps the two of them together, harnessing different aspects of the Scottish psyche, the driven tee-total engineer alongside the gallus romantic, afraid of no-one, might just have pulled it off.

For sources I used both Ken Gallacher's and Tom Miller's biographies of Jim Baxter, as well as the Jim Baxter Story DVD and the more recent BBC Alba documentary. For the Scotland matches and the authentic press and player reaction I drew upon "Scotland in the Sixties" by Ronnie McDevitt. For background stats I was able to return to the ever helpful "Wee red book" and David Docherty's, "The Rangers Football companion". I did want to tell Walter Skocic's real background story but did not know how to find him. I wrote to the Austrian FA, explaining the premise of my book and asking if they could connect me with Walter or his family but I received no reply. I believe he is still alive aged 83. I would like to ask him if he is sorry for breaking Jim Baxter's leg.

I tried contacting Rangers TV, where I explained that Tom Miller might like to see my book. I had hoped that Tom may have given me a chance to let Jim Baxter's family see what I had written before I published this account. I have contacted Empics to ask permission to use the pictures.

I had previously read"The Ghost of White Hart Lane; In search of my father the football legend" by Rob White and Julie Welch and kept its details in mind for the World Cup semi-final chapter. Such was the strength of Scottish football at the time, you could plausibly split another second in July 1964 and have John White glance at the tree as he continues to run for the clubhouse. White and Baxter combined exceptionally for Scotland, they played together in 12 matches and Scotland were never beaten over 90minutes in any of these games. Scotland won 10, drew with West Germany away and lost only to Czechoslovakia in extra time when White and Baxter were in the same team. England were beaten three out of three and Scotland scored 36 conceding 15 over the 12 games. This wasn't because Scotland were consistently victorious between November 1960(Baxter's first game) and May 1964(White's final game) in the eleven games the pair did not combine in Scotland won 5 and lost 6 with a goal difference of 28-27. If White and Baxter had both been available for the qualifying games for the 1966 World Cup and for the consequent Finals, statistically, Scotland would have won every game 3-1!

I have been asked why I did not explore the wider societal implications of Scotland winning the World Cup in 1966. I have no doubt it would have increased Scottish national self-confidence and amplified our profile across the world but I was writing a football book and not a political one. That's the beauty of alternative history, you can let your own mind imagine what might have happened next.

It has been hugely enjoyable to write this book. I know these players far better than I know the current generation. It has been a delight to give them back the fine margin that worked against them in 1964/5 and provide them with the World Cup stage they would surely have graced so well. I hope it has been as enjoyable to read.

Martin Dey
September 2023

Bonus Story: 1966/67. When Scottish football was the best in Europe. Fact!

If you believe it is completely far fetched that Scotland could have won the World Cup in 1966 read on.

The Scottish League is sneered upon in England. Apart from Rangers excellent recent run to the Europa LeagueFinal, results in Europe are often a disappointment with some teams going out before the schools go back. It was not always like this. When I was growing up in the 1960s and early 70s the list of countries whose clubs I expected Scottish teams to beat was so long that it would be quicker to say that only Italian, West German, English and Spanish teams were rated higher in my estimation and even then we could always give them a good go.

Scottish club football was not just good in the 1960s, in 1966/67 it was the best in Europe. This is a statistical fact and it should be better known and celebrated. I am not simply saying this because Celtic won the premier European competition but basing the statement on all competitive matches played in Europe that season, European Cup, Cup Winner's Cup and Fairs Cup. How else can you compare the strength of different leagues except to aggregate how each country did across these three tournaments? If today's TV money was allocated according to this co-efficient, then the Scottish League would be coining it in in 1966/67!

If you take every game played in European competition that season and apply two points for a win, one for a draw, none for a defeat, as was in force in all leagues at the time, you emerge with Scotland topping the table. An even greater achievement when it is recalled that Scotland had fewer entries than bigger countries, who had more teams in the Fairs Cup and countries with last year's winners returning. Celtic won the European Cup, Rangers lost narrowly in the Final of the Cup Winners Cup and Kilmarnock reached the semi-finals of the Fairs Cup. Dundee United punched above their weight with home and away victories over Barcelona and a home win over Juventus. Dunfermline helped the overall Scottish score with home and away wins over Frigg Oslo and a home win over Dynamo Zagreb. Although I have not calculated other seasons in a similar fashion, I am sure that Scotland will be the country with the smallest population with a claim to being the best in Europe in any given season since European cup competition began.

European Cup

Scotland	p9 pts 15
Italy	p10 pts 15
Bulgaria	p11 pts 13

Czechoslovakia p8 pts 12

Cup winners Cup

West Germany p11 pts 15

Scotland p9 pts 12

Belgium p10 pts 11

Bulgaria p8 pts 7

Fairs Cup

Italy p22 pts 33

England p22 pts 27

Scotland p16 pts 23

Yugoslavia p18 pts 18]

Combined Total.

1. Scotland p 34 pts 50
2. Italy p34 pts 49
3. England p31 pts 37
4. West Germany p27 pts 36
5. Belgium p29 pts 28
6. Yugoslavia p27 pts 27
7. Spain p27 pts 26
8. East Germany p16 pts 22
9. Hungary p16 pts 18
10. Holland p 17 pts 17

(I was unable to edit this table in kindle create after downloading it. Bulgaria were in 9th place with played 19 points 20. Holland with young Johan Cruyff, Wim Van Hanegem et al are not yet in the top 10 but soon will be)

The Scottish League's record is not bad from a League that was every year exporting hundreds of its best players and prospects to English clubs. During the 1960s a Scottish League select annually played an English League select (strangely and somewhat arrogantly called "The Football League"). The results from the mid

60s were:

1964: Football League 2-2 Scottish League

1965: Scottish League 2-2 Football League

1966: Football League 1-3 Scottish League

1967: Scottish league 0-3 Football League.

Level pegging. I am sure if the best XI from each league played each other now, four years in a row, it would be 4 victories for the English Premier League (presuming it is no longer the "Football Premier League"!)

No Scottish team lost at home in Europe in 1966/67 and Scotland beat World Champions England at Wembley, ending England's 19 game unbeaten run. Truly, it was a good time to be a Scottish football supporter back in 1966/67.

The Scottish results in Europe that season:

Celtic (European Cup): picture at start of article.

Celtic 2-0 Zurich (Gemmell McBride)

Zurich 0-3 Celtic (Gemmell 2 McBride)

Nantes 1-3 Celtic (McBride Lennox Chalmers)

Celtic 3-1 Nantes (Johnstone Lennox Chalmers)

Vojvodina 1-0 Celtic

Celtic 2-0 Vojvodina (Chalmers McNeil)

Celtic 3-1 Dukla Prague (Johnstone Wallace 2)

Dukla 0-0 Celtic

Celtic 2-1 Inter Milan (Gemmell Chalmers)

Sepp Maier drops the ball after jumping into a static Roger Hynd and Hynd scores the goal that would have won the Cup for Rangers in normal time. However, Franz Beckenbauer is poised to tell the referee the decision he wants.

Rangers(European Cup Winners Cup)

Glentoran 1-1 Rangers (McLean)

Rangers 4-0 Glentoran (Johnston D. Smith Setterington McLean)

Rangers 2-1 Borussia Dortmund (Johansen Smith,A)

Borussia 0-0 Rangers

Rangers 2-0 Zaragossa (Smith Willoughby)

Zaragossa 2-0 Rangers (Rangers win toss of coin)

Slavia Sofia 0-1 Rangers (Wilson)

Rangers 1-0 Slavia (Henderson)

Bayern Munich 1-0 Rangers

Kilmarnock (Fairs Cup)

Antwerp 0-1 Kilmarnock (McInally)

Kilmarnock 7-2 Antwerp (McInally 2, Queen 2, McLean 2 Watson)

Kilmarnock 1-0 La Gantoise (Murray)

La Gantoise 1-2 Kilmarnock (McInally McLean)

Lokomotiv Leipzig 1-0 Kilmarnock

Kilmarnock 2-0 Lokomotiv (McFadzean McIlroy)

Leeds 4-2 Kilmarnock (McIlroy 2)

Kilmarnock 0-0 Leeds

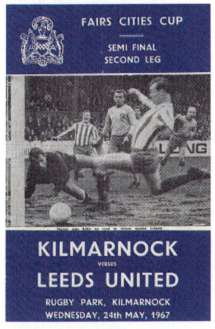

Dunfermline (Fairs Cup)

Frigg 1-3 Dunfermline (Fleming 2 Callaghan)

Dunfermline 3-1 Frigg (Delaney 2 Callaghan)

Dunfermline 4-2 Dynamo Zagreb (Delaney Edwards Ferguson 2)

Dynamo Zagreb 2-0 Dunfermline (Zagreb won toss of coin)

Dundee United (Fairs Cup)

Barcelona 1-2 Dundee United (Hainey Seeman)

Dundee United 2-0 Barcelona (Mitchell Hainey)

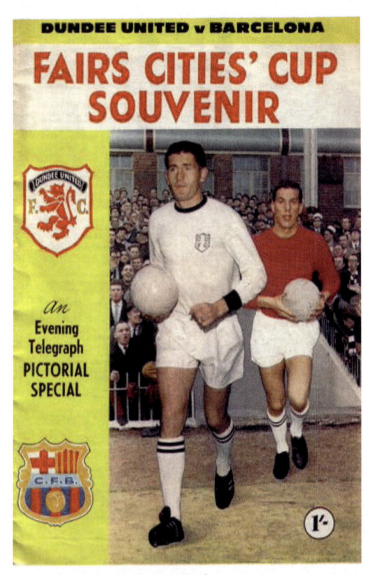

Juventus 3-0 Dundee United

Dundee United 1-0 Juventus (Dossing)

PRAISE FOR AUTHOR

Great story, language and historical context. I loved this book. Makes you think about Isobel and many others as real women and what happens when people are picked out as deviant by oppressors.

A historical detective story that will keep the reader on the edge of their seat. Bringing to life the people of post civil war scotland and exploring their superstitions and prejudices.

This is a fast paced read, part historical detective story and part mystery. I found this novel a poignant comment on the prejudices, superstitions and downright injustices of 17th century Scotland. Laced with traditional faery and folk beliefs and written in authentic dialect of place and time, this was an enthralling read. Highly recommended.

- WORLDWIDE REVIEWS OF "ISOBEL GOWDIE:ALAS THAT I SHOULD COMPARE HIM TO A MAN"

I cried. This incredible book. I fell in love with the characters. I always want the Scots to win. I learned so much. It really did make me cry and that may be why I liked it so much.

Could not put this book down. I read endless historical fiction both as an escape and for perspective. This single work provided pleasure, *insight and desire to have more.*

I had to pry myself away. It is the reason we read. Books such as this.

- WORLDWIDE REVIEWS OF "NO GREAT MISCHIEF IF THEY FALL"

I am a voracious reader, though a picky one. I can really only tolerate books where I am held captive by the writing and the characters. This book has done both. I read and read, then became despondent when I finished. I loved this book. Thank you for such a thrilling journey.

Immersed in history, geopolitics and loyalties, a great read that sticks with you. I was immersed in the sense of place, time and history. You can feel the author's need for authenticity. there are moments of elation and those of nerve wracking trauma. This would be magnificent on screen.

- WORLDWIDE REVIEWS OF "LIBERTY OR DEATH"

Another great story by Martin Dey. The last of the trilogy is poignant and insightful. The creative concept of a soldier surviving four brutal wars spanning so many years makes the trilogy well worth reading and it would make a terrific television series.

I have thoroughly enjoyed the series. the finale, like the other two books, has a great plot woven into historical events. A great read.

- WORLDWIDE REVIEWS OF "THE WORLD TURNED UPSIDE DOWN."

BOOKS BY THIS AUTHOR

Isobel Gowdie: Alas That I Should Compare Him To A Man

Isobel Gowdie creates magic with her words. Isobel is a bard whose ballads brighten the dark winter's gloom. She is a healer, curser and dreamer. Her dreams lift her far above her life of hard subsistence toil. They let her soar above the ordinary. Until men call her witch. As Isobel languishes in her cell, a Public Notary arrives from Edinburgh with a commission to investigate. Archie Kellas is a veteran of the recent bloody civil war, an enemy of the local lairds. As Archie seeks answers he must overcome the lairds' hostility and the bewildering complexity of Isobel's extraordinary words. Can Archie uncover the truth before Isobel is consigned to the flames?

No Great Mischief If They Fall

In 1745 young Ewan MacKenzie is caught up in Bonnie Prince Charlie's Jacobite Rebellion and sees his home destroyed by redcoat soldiers as they pacify the Highlands. Yet 12 years later Ewan becomes a redcoat himself. "No Great Mischief If They Fall" explores why a man might make such a transition, while following Ewan's service with the 78th Fraser Highlanders from the siege of Louisbourg to the battle for Quebec. Ewan faces many dangers, none more so than when he finds himself in the same army as the redcoat who harmed his family.

Liberty Or Death

Ewan MacKenzie has survived the Jacobite Rebeliion and the French and Indian War but even these bitter conflicts do not prepare him for the terror and divided allegiance he is yet to face. The terror comes when he is a captive of the Seneca, while Pontiac's Rising ignites the frontier. Divided loyalty comes when 12 years later war looms between Britain and Ewan's adoptive home of America. How could a man fight against comrades he once swore an oath to serve alongside?

The World Turned Upside Down

Ewan MacKenzie drags his injured and weary body through the great American Revolutionary War battles of Brandywine, Germantown and Monmouth, while also having to endure the harsh winter camps at Morristown and Valley Forge, yet his time of greatest fear and guilt arises when his home and family are threatened by the British invasion of Virginia, with Ewan's sworn enemy, Malachi Cobden, in their midsts. An enthralling conclusion to the trilogy of stories charting Ewan's eventful life.

Printed in Great Britain
by Amazon

36185322R00086